RETRIBUTION MAN

Shaun A J Wright

Text copyright © Shaun Wright 2021

Retribution Man was written Shaun A J Wright.

Shaun A J Wright has asserted his right to be identified as the author of this work in accordance with the copyright, Designs and Patents Act 1988.

All rights reserved. No part of this work may be reproduced or utilised in any form or by any means, electronic or mechanical, including photocopying, recording, or by any information storage and retrieval system, without the prior written consent of the publishers.

This is a work of fiction. All characters and descriptions of events are products of the author's imagination and any resemblance to actual persons is entirely coincidental.

ISBN: 9798740106700

To Guy and Jamie

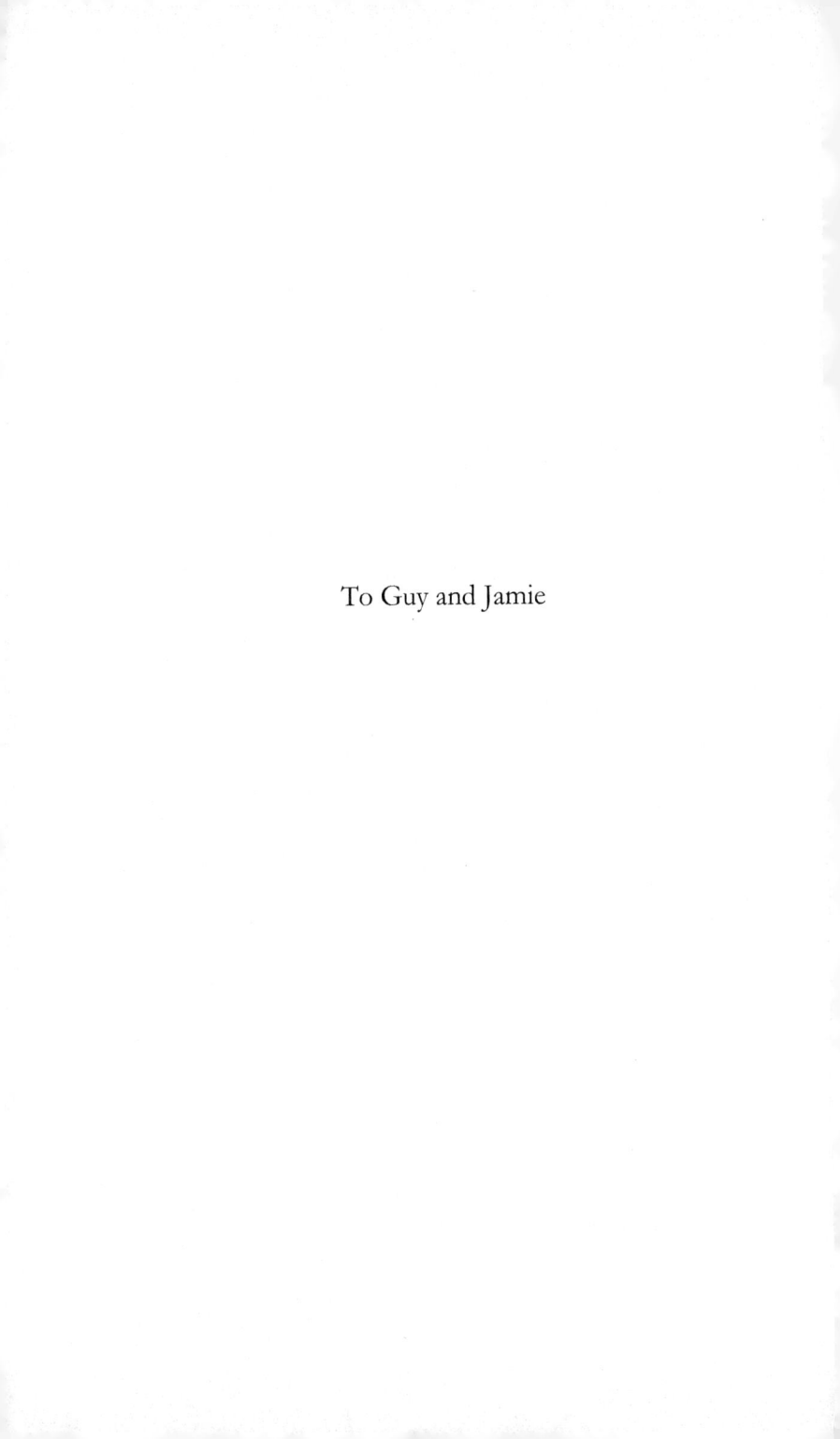

Chapter 1

The day for Chief Detective Dan Liebenberg started like most days. Arriving in the car park, he would park his 20-year-old, green, Buick LeSabre car, in his usual place, then walk across to the main entrance of the Harrisburg police bureau. The bureau was an unassuming, brick faced, three-story building located in the middle of Harrisburg.

Harrisburg was the state capital of Pennsylvania and situated on the Susquehanna River. The city wasn't as big as the surrounding cities such as Philadelphia, Baltimore, or Pittsburgh, all within a few hours' drive. Like other cities in the area, the large steel mills that helped build its economic fortunes, were now long-gone, a distant memory. In recent years, as the result of mismanagement and corruption, the City Council had struggled balancing its books. Key government services and departments had been downsized to reflect the financial strain and the Harrisburg police bureau had not escaped.

Arriving in the reception area, always a buzz of activity, Dan said a few 'good mornings' to the familiar group of people, some of whom had worked there even longer than him. He then took an elevator to the third floor and found his office at the back of the building to settle-down for the day's work. This consisted of opening post, checking emails and catching-up with the latest events that may have taken place overnight.

Dan had been heading-up the Harrisburg Major Crimes and Homicide Division for over twenty-five years now. Their patch covered the surrounding towns and rural areas, of which Harrisburg was one of the largest. The nature of the crimes that took place were mostly petty crime and domestic related, not the 'serious' organised crimes like the ones that you would find in the underworld of the larger cities. However, there was always something of a criminal nature going on and it kept them busy. If they needed support, they knew that their colleagues in the bigger cities would help them out.

He was now sixty-three years of age and had been working at the Harrisburg police bureau since the age of twenty. He had been married and divorced on two occasions before finally accepting that a man in his position, with his demanding workload, could never have a successful marriage, well, not one that lasted. He realised that marriage and his career were like mixing beer with milk. You may try it once or twice, then you realise they don't go together so you try and avoid it.

He was now specialising in remaining single, however, he was more than happy to let his defences down for any 'loose' ladies who may want to take advantage of his good nature, his 'never say no' personality or his accommodating bed-side manner.

He was due to go into retirement in two months. However, on two occasions now, they had persuaded him to stay for an extra year or two. There was talk about the department being restructured again, or integrated into another, so the possibility of them asking him to stay on this time round was highly unlikely.

His passion in life was the chase, the buzz of catching another crook or solving a challenging crime. For someone who was constantly on the go for the past forty years, he was dreading what retirement had in store for him.

Chapter 2

The Harrisburg major crime and homicide division consisted of a team of dedicated crime fighters. No job was too big, or small, for them to tackle.

Dan's faithful partner, Mike 'Rico' Eyre, was in his early sixties and had been working alongside him for over twenty years now. Besides working together, they were also the best of friends. Their Friday night drinking sessions were legendary, full of sexist, bigoted remarks and for most rookies in the department, to be avoided at all costs.

They were once involved with a high-speed boat chase down the Susquehanna River. As a result, they were dubbed the 'Sonny and Rico' of the mighty Harrisburg crime fighting team, without the sharp suits, fast cars, and speed boats that one would associate with the Miami Vice television series. There were at least three Mikes running around the Harrisburg police bureau at any one time, so he was always called Rico when on duty, chasing criminals.

He was another serial divorcee, managing three successful divorces, having at least three children that he knew of. He was constantly broke, as most of his monthly salary evaporated once he received it. He could hardly afford to live on his own, so sharing his life with another was not an option, that's if he wanted to. Like Dan, his whole life consisted of chasing low-life scum as he knew of no other career choice.

Harry Edwards, was another well-established member of the division, having been with the team for around thirty years now. He had managed to stay married, unlike his colleagues, which was a first for the division. He had been shot three times now, each in a different part of his body. Dan and Rico liked having him around, as their chances of getting shot were potentially minimised.

The team were held together by Irene Smith, a petite blonde in her early sixties, who controlled and co-ordinated all the daily activities. She was desk-bound and did all the legwork, the background checks on the various databases, the stuff that most male detectives either didn't have the patience to do or simply knew she would do a better job than they could. She would also, at times, offer alternative ideas or solutions to a crime that most of the men sitting in the room hadn't thought of.

Irene knew that most of the men in the police department would like to spend at least 20 passionate minutes with her. However, she was a smart, streetwise cookie with a sharp sense of humour which would quickly deflate most men's egos and keep their advances in check. In any case, she had been married for close to 30 years and was more than happy with what she had.

No major crimes had been reported in Harrisburg and the surrounding areas for the past few weeks now, so there hadn't been much action lately, no good cases to investigate or solve. For the team, it looked like another day of trying to look occupied to satisfy their superiors.

Chapter 3

As per usual, when Dan arrived at his desk, Irene had a cup of coffee waiting for him. He greeted her in his usual fashion, "Hi gorgeous, if I was only 10 years younger." he said, admiring how her jeans emphasised her butt.

To which she would reply, "Dream on, make it 20" and they'd both laugh.

The call came through at 08.30, relayed from the front desk to Irene. She introduced herself. The voice on the phone said:

"Irene, listen to me carefully now. Mad Max Montana is presently in room 104 at the Gardens Motel, north of Harrisburg. He did the job at the Rivonia. If you want to catch him, then you better move fast. Pass on the message to Dan Liebenberg straight away."

The caller hung-up, not leaving his name. Irene, and every major crime division in a five-hundred-mile radius, knew the name. She instantly realised the importance of the call. She turned around to the rest of the team.

"You wanna catch Mad Max Montana? Well here's your chance, and you owe me a drink sometime." she said, as she put the message down on Dan's desk. Everyone had heard the message, they knew who Mad Max was, and so all looked up from their computers to face Dan, knowing that their day was about to change rapidly.

Dan looked at the message, and said out loud, "Gents, get your jackets, Mad Max Montana is in town and it appears he may have done a job at the Rivonia, let's get going." He added, "Treat this as a category one and don't compromise your safety. We need weapons, full bullet proof protection and a door-buster. We are on the road in five minutes, go, go, go."

After the immediate adrenaline buzz had kicked in, there was a frantic rush around the office to get the necessary equipment, with officers repeatedly checking that their gun mechanisms were working and making sure their body armour was correctly fitted. They knew Max would be armed and dangerous. They didn't call him Mad Max because of any mental illness, but for his ruthless, cold-blooded nature, a known killer in the underworld of the Philadelphia and Baltimore areas.

Chapter 4

The Gardens Motel, located fifteen minutes north of Harrisburg, was the typical overnight convenient stop found throughout the USA. It provided basic accommodation for the out-of-town businessman or family passing through. Located alongside the Interstate 81, the motel was a single-floor, L-shaped building now showing its age. It was ideal for someone wanting to keep a low profile.

Dan and the team arrived at the Gardens Motel, parking their cars around the corner, out-of-sight of room 104. In single file, they advanced to the top of the stairs, where room 104 was located.

The officers then moved to each side of the door, whilst the officer in-charge of breaking down the door, the 'door-basher', positioned his hydraulic ram horizontally in the middle of the door frame. With a few manual pumps on the lever, the door frame suddenly snapped with a loud bang.

Mad Max Montana had been lying on his bed, with his gun alongside him on the side-table. At any moment, he was expecting to meet three gentlemen, also carrying guns, so he was tense and anxious. Having heard the sudden loud bang coming from the door, he flew off the bed and picked up his gun, all in-one go, and in an instant, shot four bullets towards the door. All the bullets went straight through the cheap, motel door and then ricocheted off the walls of the stairwell. The bullets missed all the police officers, who had been positioned on each side of the door.

Knowing that you are being shot at focuses the mind in an instant, and this was no exception. The shock to their senses was swift, with their hearts now pounding like steam trains. Dan stared at his fellow officers, and said, 'Jesus.'

When it appeared that there were no more shots, Dan then said, "This is the Police, put down your gun."

After a few seconds, a voice from behind the door said "Okay, come in."

One forceful kick later and the door sprung open, and the police were inside the room. Inside was the legendary Mad Max, who had been taken by surprise and already laid his gun to the side and had lifted his hands to his head, accepting that his last two bullets in his gun were no match for the fifty bullets pointing at him. He may be called Mad Max, but he was sane enough to realise when the odds were stacked up against him.

"What the hell are the police doing in my room?" he thought.

Max was forced onto the floor, placed on his stomach, and handcuffed. Once he was patted down, they lifted him and took him out of the bedroom, down the steps, and into a waiting police car.

Dan and Rico had a quick look around the bedroom, and realised that although they had Max, there did not appear to be a significant amount of money in the room. In fact, there was no indication of him having any proceeds or evidence linking him to a crime. Dan looked at Rico and said, "We have no evidence, other than a message."

Dan saw Rico leaving the room and had a good idea where he was going. He joined him outside and there he was having a stress-relieving cigarette. Rico offered him a cigarette, he lit it and took one long drag on it. The relief was swift as the smoke filled his lungs, and his shaking slowed. Dan had given up smoking ten years ago, however, he occasionally had a relapse and Rico always knew when this would happen. There appeared to be some link between being shot at and then having a cigarette.

All Max's possessions such as his overnight bag, his cell phone, and the gun were collected, and they set off for the bureau.

The most important thing was that they had big, bad Mad Max in custody, the challenge now was to find a crime and make the charges stick. They also needed to find out what the Rivonia job was all about.

When they got back into the office, Max was checked into the finest room that the Harrisburg police bureau could offer. He knew what the inside of a prison cell looked like, having previously spent several nights in these establishments.

The team congregated back in the office and Irene gave Dan a wink, and said "I told you," as if she was totally responsible for the capture of Mad Max.

"You think you're so smart, don't you, you smug cow," and the rest of the team laughed.

Dan addressed everyone in the office, "Right, we have Mad Max sitting in the pen. Besides a message that we received earlier informing us his whereabouts, we don't have a crime to link him to."

"The four bullets that were fired from his gun were aimed at our police officers, meaning he's up for armed assault, which should take him down for a few years. However, let's not count on it, he could manage to get off this one again."

Dan looked at Irene and asked. "Have we heard about this Rivonia job yet?" She shook her head in denial.

"Could it be the Rivonia casino?" said Harry.

A call came through and Irene picked up the phone. She then signalled to Dan and said quietly, with her hand over the telephone mouthpiece, "The Rivonia," and pointed to his phone.

Dan picked up the receiver. The call was from James Turner, the General Manager of the Rivonia Golf Club and Casino, who he had met on a few occasions.

He said, "Hi Dan, it looks like we had a break-in sometime overnight, can you please come over and have a look, thanks."

Dan put down the phone, looked up, and said to his team, "Gents, get your jackets on, we're off to the Rivonia casino."

Chapter 5

The Rivonia Golf Club and Casino was situated in the country, forty miles north of Harrisburg. Everyone conveniently called it 'the Rivonia'. Through the manned entrance gate there was a long, meandering, attractive drive up to club house, the road was lined with tall fir trees positioned at regular intervals along the entire length. The club house was charmingly situated, with a large terrace overlooking an attractive pond and a fountain in the middle. The golf course extended as far as the eye could see. On most sunny days, it would where you would find most guests having a relaxing drink or something to eat, that is, if they had managed to venture out of the dark confines of the casino area.

The main area of the club consisted of an A framed building housing the common areas such as the main lobby, reception, and restaurant areas. The building had few attractive features and now showed its age. Alongside the main section was the casino area, with its dark interior and bright, flashing lights. There were also two annexes that extended from the main area where the guest bedrooms were located. All the main areas and guest bedrooms were at ground-floor level.

The original site, dating back to the sixties, had started off as a golf club with some restaurant facilities. In the eighties, the owners had added fifty bedrooms and a large banqueting hall. On most weekends, besides the local golf tournaments that regularly took place, there were now also weddings and other social functions.

In the nineties, the owners had decided to change the banqueting hall into a casino area which now contained around 30 slot machines and a few roulette, black-Jack, and poker tables. It was a small-scale casino establishment, at least when compared to the some of the larger ones in the surrounding cities.

For the hard-working locals of Harrisburg and the smaller towns in the surrounding Pennsylvania county, the Rivonia was well known and frequented by many golfers and 'would-be' professional gamblers aspiring to turn their weekend hobby into a full-time occupation.

The venue was a family-run business, having been in the Jackson family for over three generations now. It was obvious that significant investment would be needed soon, however for the locals, it provided an escape from their boring lives and it was adequate for their needs.

Chapter 6

From the outside, room 212 looked the same as every other bedroom in the club, however, it had a different internal layout as there were no beds inside. The room had been converted into a secure room when they built the casino. To guests or visitors, it just looked like any other room and no-one, besides a select few of management staff, knew that the safe secure room existed. The room was divided into two separate sections. One was used as a safe money storage section, a highly secure area where the money from all the club's commercial activities was kept. This included the winnings from the casino, the takings from the bar, the two restaurants and revenue from the overnight stays.

The other half was an office area consisting of two desks. One desk was where the money was counted and bundled every morning, the other was where the central CCTV monitoring station for the hotel was located. This system was for recording purposes only, it wasn't permanently manned. The monitoring of the CCTV was done in the reception and the duty manager's office.

The safe secure section of the room lay behind a heavy-duty steel mesh partition wall, extending from the floor to the ceiling. Access to the area was through a single door with a high-specification double-lock security system.

Within the confines of the secure room were seven vertical secure boxes, which were used to collect and store the money. These money boxes stood 4ft high and 2ft square and mounted on wheels, so that they could be conveniently transported between the various areas of the club.

The lid of each money box had the day of the week stencilled-in, so the duty manager knew which one to use when they were collecting the takings for the day. At the end of the evening, usually around midnight, when the casino and most of the bars and restaurants were closed, the duty manager, with the security manager in tow, would go around and empty the contents of all the tills. Having collected all the takings, the money box was then transported back to room 212, where it was stored in the secure safe area for the night. This procedure was done every night.

Fidelity Armed Transit Services, a local Harrisburg company, would pick up the money every Monday morning and deliver the contents to the local bank.

Chapter 7

Dan and his team arrived and parked the car in the hotel car park. They then went to the reception area where they met with James, the General Manager, and Andy, the Security manager. They walked through the lobby area, then advanced down the corridor into room 212, where they were shown through the door. In front of him, on the left-side of the room, was the secure safe area, which had been previously opened by James. It contained seven money boxes with their lids forcibly opened. Upon closer inspection, it was obvious that their contents were missing.

"How much?" asked Dan, looking at James.

"Around $1.4 million," said James.

"Holy cow." said Dan, glancing at Rico. He looked around the room and at the steel mesh partition wall. There appeared to be no signs of forced entry into the area. Looking up at the ceiling showed a ventilation grille, everything appeared to be in place. Furthermore, he noted that there were no ceiling tiles that could have been lifted to gain entry.

Dan turned to James and asked, "Can you please run through what you did when you entered the room this morning?"

James described in detail what he did, "As usual, I took out the two keys, one to open the main door into the room, the other for the penned-off secure area door. Having opened the door, I switched on the main light and then went over to open the secure area door and that was when I found the empty money boxes."

Dan interrupted him, "The secure door was definitely locked?"

"Yes," said James, "the key had been sitting in the main duty managers' office safe for the past twelve hours."

"Who else had access to these keys for the room?" said Dan.

"Well, there are the two duty managers who have the code for the office safe, which contains the keys for Room 212." He added, "The owner, Peter Jackson, has a spare set of keys which he keeps in his own safe."

Dan turned around to survey the crime scene again and said quietly, "How the hell did they get into this secure area?"

He looked at Rico and they both smiled, both thinking the same thing. This robbery looked to be an inside-job.

Chapter 8

A sudden cry rang out from down the passage, and everyone stopped what they were doing and looked at each other, puzzled. They left room 212 to investigate the cry for help.

In front of room 215, the guest bedroom two doors down, a Mexican chambermaid with limited English was crying and pointing in the direction of the room.

James was just about to enter the door, but Dan touched him on the shoulder, signalling him to stand back while he entered first. Dan took out his gun, slowly pushed the door open and cautiously entered the room. Rico, gun drawn, followed his partner into the room.

The room was clear of any other human beings, well, living ones. They were shocked to come across not one, but two dead bodies, both male and lying on the same bed. The bodies were mostly covered by a blanket. Both had a single gunshot wound through their foreheads.

Upon closer inspection, there appeared to be a lot of blood surrounding their eyes. Dan reached over and with two fingers, lifted and parted the eyelids. What he saw made him recoil backward, bumping into Rico directly behind him. The eyeballs had been removed from the two victims.

"Oh my god," he said, looking at Rico, "I've never seen that before." Rico nodded; his stare fixed on the victims faces.

Dan slowly drew back the blanket, revealing that both bodies were naked. He noted that besides their missing eyes, all the fingers had been removed. It appeared that all the detached body parts were missing and had been removed from the scene.

"What the hell has been going on here, then?" said Rico, in amazement.

Looking around the rest of the room, they noticed the word 'bastard' written in lipstick on the mirror. Rico looked at Dan, "Could this be a gay revenge killing?" Dan nodded in agreement.

The bedroom had two beds, a double bed, containing the two bodies, and a single that appeared to be unslept in. Besides the two dead bodies, there was nothing else in the room, such as personal clothing or belongings. No overnight bags or mobile telephones that most people would have when staying in a hotel. It appeared that everything had been intentionally removed from the scene, including four eyeballs and twenty fingers.

Dan turned around and went back to the entrance door, he informed everyone that this was now a murder investigation scene, and that the area was to be sectioned off. They were all in a state of shock and left the area to tell their colleagues of the recent events.

Dan re-entered the room, turned to Rico and said, "We better call in forensics."

"No-shit, Kojak." said Rico, as they both smiled.

Their immediate thoughts were that there must be some link between the stolen $1.4 million and the murder scene in front of them. However, their only potential suspects were dead, and they had neither their eyeballs nor fingers.

With no signs of forced entry, no clothing, and no form of personal identification, this was going to be a challenging case for them and forensics.

They went back to room 212 and had another look around. Once again, it looked like a no-evidence crime scene.

Dan said to Rico, "Are we looking at one or two crime scenes here?"

Rico responded with, "Who knows."

Once Natalie King from forensics arrived, Dan and Rico knew it was time to head back to the bureau. Natalie was a feisty number, who took no prisoners, so to speak, and was feared by most hardened policemen. Normal pleasantries, such as a smile, were a rarity, and she typically barked orders at you. Some suggested that her dad was German, an ex-gestapo officer, and one could imagine her teaching foxtrot dancing lessons to a group of elite SS commanders.

Some suggested that perhaps Rico had broken her heart once, but he would neither confirm nor deny this fact.

It was two o'clock now, and as they were wanting to interview Mad Max before going home for the evening, they headed back to the bureau.

Chapter 9

Back in the bureau, with Irene, the team congregated in the crime investigation briefing room. They sat down and faced the blank briefing board before them. In the next few days, this board would quickly be filled with all sorts of facts and pictures about the case.

Their crime-busting juices were bubbling, and they were all eager to get this show on the road. They had two crimes to solve, and they knew Mad Max was linked to them somehow. He was finally going to be nailed and put away for a long time.

Dan started the briefing. "Right, we appear to have two crime scenes here. In room 212, we have what looks to be a robbery of the Rivonia casino takings. It seems to me that it may be an inside job as there were no signs of forced entry into the area."

"The other consists of a murder scene in room 215, comprising of two naked male occupants, killed with a single bullet to their heads. There was a written message on the mirror, saying 'bastard' suggesting that it may be a motive of sexual jealousy."

"However, the precise method of the killing may also suggest that it could be an organised hit. Gents, for the meantime, let's treat these crime scenes as two separate incidents that appear to have happened on the same night, within metres of each other."

Irene always wondered why, even with a woman in the room, he always referred to everyone as gents, still, it was good to be considered one of the boys, in a weird sort of way.

"We also have Mad Max in our bureau who appears to be connected, with the casino job and possibly the murder of the victims as well."

Rico added, "We've been wanting to nail this bastard for years now, let's see what he has to say."

Chapter 10

Max Montana was commonly known in the underworld, and every police bureau in the area, as 'Mad Max'. The Montana family were Italian immigrants, who had always been associated with organised crime in the Philly area, and Max was another product of the dynasty. It was obvious he would be a psychologist's dream, as he displayed most of the range of personality disorders known to man, principally that of a sadistic psychopath.

It was common knowledge that any criminal activity, involving drugs, prostitution, and night-club security within a three-hundred-mile radius of Philly would have some connection to Mad Max.

He knew that in his chosen profession, reputation meant everything, and the eviller the punishment that he dealt out, the more respect he would receive. There had been rumours of him cutting off people's ears, then sending them to those considering being a trial witness against him. He would often record victims, especially his competitors, being brutally beaten up and then send the video to other third parties. Most in the underworld of the Philly and Baltimore areas feared him, and they knew to stay clear of him and his associates.

Most cops would confirm that as he always got others to carry out the 'dirty' work, and no-one ever 'squealed' on him, they could never pin anything on him. Most of his associates in crime were sitting in various prisons around the local counties, but Mad Max had not experienced a long spell inside a prison cell yet.

At the age of sixty-eight, he knew his time in the spotlight was coming to an end, and there was always a younger, meaner bastard ready to fill his shoes. His criminal activities had been slowing down, especially after he survived a 'hit' from a Russian gangster who had wanted to take over his patch. Three bullets had entered various parts of his body, but none provided the fatal blow, which most would consider a crying shame.

He had spent the previous night in the Garden Motel, located near the Rivonia.

The day had started well for him as around 7.30, he received a text message from Franco. It said, "*Rivonia job went to plan, see you at 09.00, Franco.*"

Mad Max's face had broken into a big smile. He had no idea what had been planned the previous night, or how it was executed, but it was certainly pay-day for him. He reached over and took out his Remington A360, and went through his well-established routine of checking that the internal mechanisms were working, so that nothing could go wrong.

He smiled and thought that at least one bullet will be lodged in Victor Stanley's head later that morning. He got up, had a shower, then made some coffee and waited in his room for the rendezvous. However, his day was about to get worse.

At 09.00, there was a loud cracking noise, followed by a loud bang, as the bedroom door broke. Fearing for his life and expecting the worse, he took out his gun and proceeded to empty most of its contents at the centre of the motel door. For most of his criminal life he had adopted a shoot-first policy, he could always face the consequences later. However, his actions that day would have consequences that he'd regret for the rest of his life.

Chapter 11

Mad Max was removed from his secure prison cell and escorted into the interrogation room. He was familiar with most police interrogation rooms in the Pennsylvania County; however, he had not yet had the pleasure of visiting the Harrisburg police bureau one.

The first round of questions started and from the start, it was obvious that Max was not going to be cooperative and he would maintain his silence when it suited him. As he had been in the same scenario on several instances now, he was a master at not giving them the answers they wanted.

He knew that the only thing that linked him to the Rivonia was the text message that was sent to him by Franco. Well, besides the fact that he chose to stay in a motel 20 minutes from the Rivonia on the night the crime took place, and that he had an outstanding, proven record of carrying out these types of crimes. It did occur to him that this may work against him and that those facts were certainly not going away.

Dan recognised that Mad Max was in no physical shape to have carried out the job himself, however he did have the contacts to make it happen, which was his standard playbook, getting others to do his dirty work.

"Were you at the Rivonia last night?" asked Dan.

"No." he answered.

"Were you at the Gardens motel all night?"

"Yes." he answered.

"Did you leave the motel room at any time?"

"No." he answered.

"Why did you travel 150 miles to come and stay at the Gardens motel?"

"I needed time away from the wife." he replied.

"You could afford other, nicer hotels in the area. So why did he choose a 'shit-hole' like the Gardens?" asked Rico.

"It is my favourite motel." he answered.

"Do you know about the casino job at the Rivonia that took place last night?" asked Dan.

"I know nothing about the Rivonia job." This was factually correct, as he had no idea what took place last night.

"If you had nothing to do with the crimes at the Rivonia, why did you shoot at our police officers when we arrived at your room this morning?" asked Dan.

"The door key card didn't work." answered Max. Dan looked at Rico and smiled. For a man whose reputation didn't mention a sense of humour, they thought that was quite funny. However, it could also be true.

"Do you know about the two murders that took place last night?" This question hit Max like a sledgehammer. He didn't know about the murders and decided not to answer the question.

His mind was suddenly racing overtime, besides the money that had been stolen, he had just learnt that two murders had taken place. Before he had time to digest this information, Rico asked, "Are you gay?"

Max looked up at them suddenly and told them to "Piss-off."

Dan noticed that the question seemed to rattle Max. Everyone knew he had been married to the same women for over 40 years now. However, they knew that some faithful husbands may occasionally indulge in the sexual pleasures offered by the gay community.

Once Mad Max got back into his cell, he sat on his bed, racking his brain as to what could possibly have happened at the Rivonia last night. The text from Franco this morning had confirmed that the robbery went to plan. However, two murders had taken place, suggesting that Franco had wasted both men, for whatever reason.

The text this morning also suggested that he was planning to come back to the motel to meet-up with him. However, for some strange reason, the cops had decided to spoil the party by busting down the motel door, around the same time he was meant to meet with Franco.

It appeared that Franco was on-the-run and with the money. The question was, would he ever see him or the money again? It appeared that he may had been set-up and a simple observation of his present predicament suggested that his chances of getting out of this one did not look good.

Max paced around the jail, thinking about various potential scenarios. He could not believe his luck, as his last job, a few months ago now, was supposed to be his final one. However, the Rivonia job just sounded too good to be true, so he took it on. He didn't even bother to review the plan for the job or consider that that one of his associates would runoff with money. What's more, he didn't even bother to find out who Victor Stanley was.

When Dan got back into the office area, he instructed Irene to investigate if Max had ever visited gay clubs, such as Regina's, in Philly. Regina's was a recognised venue for those who were interested in exploring an alternate lifestyle, one not necessarily of a heterosexual nature.

Chapter 12

The next morning was an early start for everyone, and they were in the briefing room at 07.00. The briefing board was slowly starting to fill up with various facts, figures, and pictures. The board had now been split into two crime headings, one for the robbery, and the other for the murders. In between the two sections was a picture of Mad Max, suggesting to anyone in the room that he had a hand in both.

Dan looked at Natalie, from forensics, and said "What have we got?" under his breath adding, "My little nest of vipers."

"Well, in the strong room, not much I'm afraid. The area shows no sign of forced entry. Most surfaces, such as the tops of the money boxes show no significant, clear fingerprints trace, suggesting that whoever did the job wore gloves, or similar. There's not much in the way of shoe prints which suggests that they wore covers over the soles."

"There are no signs of entry from the ceiling area or the main entrance door to the secure area. The lock latches on the money box lids were fastened on by rivets, and they have been drilled out and the hinges forced open. Whoever did this must have known what the latches looked like before entering the space, and what tools to bring with him. The person who drilled out the latches could be familiar with how to operate mechanical or electrical tools," she said.

She continued, "Outside the secure area, the office area doesn't appear to have been touched. I'm afraid we're scraping the bottom of the barrel with this one."

"The scene looks too clean to me and it seems that the robbery was an inside-job," she added.

"The bedroom murder crime scene is also proving to be a challenge. We have no primary evidence, such as recognised identification, like wallets containing credit cards or driver ID's. Furthermore, there are no overnight belongings or toiletries that could give us potential clues.

"Their fingers were removed, providing us with no obvious fingerprint identification. The fingers appeared to have been sheared off, a clean-cut with some compression of the outer skin, suggesting they used garden plant cutters or metal shears, or a similar tool.

"Also, the removal of the eyeballs provides us with a further challenge to positively identify the victims. These eyeballs appear to be removed by forcing out the eyeball from the socket, and then carefully cutting the attachments with a very sharp blade, like a 'Stanley knife'. This was done after the killings." Most in the room considered this a relief to hear.

She added, "Besides one or two common tattoos, an appendix scar, and old scars to the faces, we have nothing to work on.

"Oh, there was a fresh bloody, scratch on one of the suspect's upper arm, suggesting that he may have caught it on something.

"Unfortunately, we don't do toe-prints of people's feet, which in this case may have been helpful," she said, jokingly.

"Dental imprints have been taken, however if the suspects aren't from the local area, I'd be surprised if we come up with anything. We have also taken strands of hair for samples and we can check for possible DNA matches on the universal database."

Natalie carried on, "The appearance of two naked men in bed together may suggest that they were gay. However, no signs of semen were found. This missing evidence doesn't necessary mean that they were not gay."

Rico asked, "Could they have been drugged or murdered elsewhere, dragged across the room and then placed onto the bed? Were they definitely shot in place?"

She scornfully looked at him, reminding him that he had crossed the line. This was what she did for a living, and she condescendingly said, "Yes, it certainly looks like they were shot in place.

"Scanning the rest of the bedroom surfaces produced nothing. There are some prints which we are checking against the cleaner's, but they could be from the previous guest. It appears that the shooter was either in the room already or had gone into the room to catch them before their act of passion," she added.

"There are single bullet shots to each forehead, could this be a professional 'hit' job?" asked Dan.

Natalie replied, "We're not sure, until ballistics get back to us. However, the fact that they were so close to their victims suggests that they couldn't have missed their heads."

"Is there any evidence that links the murders with the casino job?" asked Dan.

Natalie shock her head and said, "At this stage, I'm afraid not."

Everyone in the room went quiet for a few moments, reflecting on the information that they had just received. Other than Mad Max, sat in his cell, they had little to go on. The only possible link they had was the message that they'd received that morning from Irene.

"Has anyone else got any other information? Harry, tell me about the CCTV monitoring system and what recordings we have."

Harry summarised that most of the public areas in the club were covered by CCTV and were in good working order. There were two car parks, one for the club guests, and the other for the public, which had direct access to the main Interstate 81 public road that goes past. The club car park was covered by CCTV and the recorded footage showed nothing untoward. The camera on the general park hadn't been working for the past few weeks now, so they had nothing on that area.

"So, what you're saying is that if our murderer was not a guest in the club and had parked their car in the general car park, we wouldn't be able to recognise the car make or registration." said Dan.

"It looks that way." replied Harry, nodding his head. "The club employed two security guards, one for the day shift, 06.00 to 16.00 and then one for the afternoon and night shift, 16.00 to 24.00. Overnight, the porter in the reception area monitors the CCTV and looks after any possible security issues. He saw nothing of concern.

"Reviewing the CCTV for the main club entrance area, between 18.00 and 24.00, there were over 150 adults who either entered or exited the main doors, which will prove a challenge spotting our possible suspect, or suspects." he said.

"We re-ran the recording for the night of the camera covering the doors to rooms 212 and 215. That camera is around ten metres away from room 212. After 23.30, when the money boxes were dropped off in room 212, there was no further activity in the area and there were no signs of anyone entering or exiting the room until 09.00 this morning.

"Two adult males, white we believe, entered Room 215 at 22.30. Then around 30 minutes later the room was entered again, this time by a single white male.

"The bedroom door was then opened again around 06.00, where a single man left with a vertical transportable luggage trolley carrying his suitcases and a hanging suit cover. The two men were not seen leaving the room. We couldn't determine whether it was the same single guy who came in after the two victims the previous evening.

"However, the images are really fuzzy and possible visual confirmation of people's faces is not possible," he added.

"Could this single person possibly be our killer?" Dan asked, looking at the others in the room.

Harry added, "Talking to the Rivonia reservations department, it appears that Room 212 was pre-booked by a Mr Victor Stanley two weeks ago, and he arrived on the Sunday afternoon around 14.00, and then checked-out at 06.00, on the Monday morning. The night porter could not remember much of him and the local CCTV cameras in area don't show a clear picture of his face as he was wearing a hat at the time of exit. As there were no car-jockeys about at that time, once he left the club entrance, there were no further trace of his movements. The murderer, and his car, simply vanished."

Various pictures taken from the CCTV recording had been pinned on to the briefing board, for all to inspect.

Dan turned to the team and said, "So, it looks like there were three persons in room 212 for most of the night, but only one came out in the morning. As the single person went into the room 30 minutes after the other two, it suggests that he could have caught them in the act, shot them, and then stayed in the room until 06.00."

Rico speculated, "He may have done this to avoid causing any suspicion. If he had left straight away with no bags, someone may have noticed him on the CCTV as it was the early hours of Monday morning with hardly anyone around."

Dan nodded, "So, he checked out the next morning with a luggage trolley, just like the rest of the guests. This all suggested that there was a degree of planning involved, that it was possibly a professional 'hit-job'. Was he then going to meet-up with Mad Max, at the motel, then drive back to Philly?"

Harry added, "Besides a couple of suitcases, there was no gear that one would expect if they were about to carry out a robbery. Well, I would have expected a step ladder, a bag of tools, or similar. It looks like an inside-job to me and no link between the two crime scenes."

"What about the other employees?" asked Dan.

Harry answered back, "Most of the senior staff are 'lifers', having worked at the club for years, and all have 'clean' records, besides some basic traffic violations. Most can vouch for where they were last night, in bed at their homes, between 24.00 and 08.00 this morning."

He added, "There were two members of staff who spent the night at the club. One was the duty manageress, Eleanor Birch, the other the night porter, Tony Smith."

Dan turned to Irene, "Not your husband, is he?"

"I wish." she said, "my husband can't steal a tenner from my purse, never mind $1.4 million." Said Irene, putting a smile on all in the room.

"Have any of them got a past record?" Said Dan.

"No, nothing that I can see," said Irene, "although, Eleanor may have financial issues as she has a poor credit score, she could have had issues paying off credit cards in the past."

"Most of us have poor credit score, some are just worse than others." said Rico, reflecting on his own credit rating.

"Something worth exploring with Ms Birch." said Dan. "What were the family and club finances like?"

Irene said, "The club and casino were turning over $1 million per week, so it appeared that it was a little 'gold-mine'. Their bank manager confirmed that there were no financial issues. There was insurance in place to cover the loss, so that may suggest a potential motive, if the owners were considering stealing the money."

"The present owners are in their early seventies. Besides, they are presently sitting on a cruise ship in the Mediterranean, suggesting that they knew nothing about it."

"Their only son, Peter, manages the present day-to-day operations, as well as other investments in the area." added Irene.

"What about the person who spends every day in the secure room and who knows exactly how much money is in that room at any one time?" said Dan.

"Lisa Brew has been the financial assistant for the past six months now. She is newly married and doesn't appear to have any major financial issues."

"Yet." said Rico, smiling.

Dan, now getting up from his chair looked at the briefing board and said. "It still looks like we have two crime scenes here, which just happened to have taken place on the same night.

"It appears that our two dead victims in room 215, were shot between 24.00 and 06.00

on Monday morning, the time when most of the staff were asleep at home in their beds. The person entering room 215 appears to be male which rules out Eleanor, but it could be Tony. However, there were still several overnight male guests in the club that need to be considered and it could be one of them.

"Most of the staff don't seem to have a motive to kill the occupants of room 215, however, most would be certainly interested in stealing $1.4 million. The motive is clear there, we just need to find out who had the opportunity to execute the theft."

He added, "We have a message linking Mad Max to the murders. As this isn't the first time he has been linked to a murder, there is a good possibility he had something to do with it."

Ricco added, "There is a saying in Philly, if there's a murder in the neighbourhood, go to Mad Max. Once he has been cleared, then you go after the other low-life scum."

Dan ended by saying, "Can we please set-up interviews with all these key staff members this afternoon?

"Also, can we find out what external contractors worked at the club, such as CCTV and air-conditioning companies?"

Chapter 13

Dan, Rico and Harry arrived back at the Rivonia around 11.00. Both areas surrounding the rooms 212 and 215 were still sealed off and the common corridor was manned by a local policeman, who was finishing his twelve-hour shift and keen to get home.

Dan thought, "Dealing with one crime scene is hard enough as it is, having two is proving a challenge, especially as they were just 10 metres apart."

Dan stepped into the secure room and looked around. He went over to the now bricked up window and looked at the cemented joints round the sides, where the existing window would have been. He knew that they couldn't possibly have come through the window. He gave the wall a push anyway, just in case it moved, but it reinforced his original opinion that it was well and truly rigid.

He looked at the secure cage area, this time focusing on the ceiling. The ventilation grille was around 3ft by 2ft square, and perhaps an adult could crawl through there. He requested a step ladder, which the handy man supplied.

Alan Stubbs, the handy man, was over 70 years in age and walked with a severe limp, suggesting that even though he had a good understanding of the club layout, he couldn't have carried out the heist, or the murders.

Alan positioned the step ladder near the ventilation discharge, climbed up the ladder, removed the grille and then climbed down. Dan then climbed up the step ladder and studied the internal ventilation ducting, which was still supplying fresh air into the area. There was a constant stream of air powerful enough to forcefully part his hair. The internal ducting directly above the grille, immediately went off at a right angle, parallel to the ceiling surface.

He put his hand in the space above the grille and pushed on a section of square ducting structure. It was rigid, suggesting that it hadn't been tampered with since the original installation. He also questioned if an adult could get around the bend of the ducting and through the grille. All this taking place while the system was still blowing fresh air into the area.

The grille was replaced into the ducting outlet.

Once out in the main corridor, Dan found the nearest ceiling access hatch. Alan once again placed the ladder beneath the hatch and went up the steps. With a special shaped

Allen-key, he twisted open the latch, which made the hatch door drop down.

Dan then climbed up the ladder, put his head inside the ceiling space, and with a flashlight, he scanned the contents of the internal area. The central section was large enough to fit an adult, however, the area was covered in ventilation ducting, hot and cold-water service pipes and electrical distribution boxes. It would be a nightmare to navigate in the dark.

Someone could have climbed in, unbolted the ventilation ducting, removed the grille, and climbed down into the area. However, his gut feeling was that the challenge was too technical for the average con. He then looked around the loft space and it was covered in spider webs, suggesting that the area had not been recently used. Also, if they had gained access into the area, someone would surely have seen the stepladder in the middle of the corridor. Furthermore, they would have been noticed on the CCTV recordings.

Once back down on the floor, he moved onto the murder scene in room 215. He had a look around, the bathroom seemed as if it had never been used, nothing had been left behind, such as soaps, shaving products, deodorants or cosmetics. The bath hadn't been used overnight. The toilet roll had been half-used, but this didn't mean that the latest occupants had used the roll.

He went into the bedroom area. The second bed, a single bed, looked as though it hadn't been slept in, unless on top of the bedding. If the murderer had slept on top of the bed until 06.00 in the morning, he had not left a strand of hair, or any shred of evidence.

He looked at the main mirror, which still had the message 'bastard' written on it. This had been done in lipstick and suggests a lover's dispute, the possible motive being jealousy. Or, it could have been done to side-track the investigation, to make them think that the crimes were not linked.

On the way out of the bedroom, he noticed another ceiling access hatch door, like the one he had just seen in the corridor. He saw that there were four screws in each corner of the hatch. He called Alan into the room and asked him why this hatch door had been screwed in. He explained that due to their age, some of the latch locks did not work, so they'd had to resort to using screws to hold the hatch door in place.

Alan then suggested that they look at the next room, room 214. They entered room 214 and positioned the step ladder directly below the hatch door. When the lid fell down, they saw two service pipes directly above the hatch opening which carried the hot and cold-water supplies to the room, and a small electrical distribution master switch for the electrics in the bedroom. Alan then pointed out the two valves, which would have needed to be isolated, if any work were to be carried out on the water systems in the bathroom.

Dan asked, "Do all the rooms have a similar layout?" Alan confirmed that this was the case.

Dan gave it some thought, could the occupants of room 215 have used the hatch to gain access to the loft area, and then enter room 212 through the grille? However, the location of the hot and cold-water pipes, directly above the access hatch door, meant it was not possible for an adult, or a child, to get access into the ceiling void.

Also, the fact that the hatch had been screwed down suggested that this was possible, but unlikely. He still believed that the robbery was an inside-job carried out by staff. The murder was a separate crime, committed by Mad Max, the motive being jealousy or a paid 'hit-job'.

Dan then asked Alan if anyone had accessed the loft spaces in the past few months. Alan looked vague and informed him that the only time they ever accessed the loft space was in the guest bedrooms, when they had to isolate the water supply, if there was a leak or they were fixing a water supply issue in the bathroom. He added that he couldn't remember when he last saw anyone in the main loft area. The maintenance of the ventilation systems, such as filter changes, were done by external contractors and they have used various vendors over the years.

Having reviewed the two scenes and found no potential evidence, Dan joined the other members of the team, who were interviewing various members of the club staff.

Chapter 14

The youngest member of the Jackson family, the heir to the dynasty, was Peter, commonly known as 'Jacko'. He was forty-five years old, and as would be expected, was well-educated and impeccably groomed. He had a passion for fast cars and wild women. It was obvious that he had been brought up on three regular meals per day and he certainly wouldn't have the telephone number of the local Chinese fast-food outlet on his speed-dial.

Where his father and uncles, who had previously run the country club, were good, honest family men with solid religious beliefs, young Jacko appeared not to have the same Jackson family mould. Some would say he was the black sheep of the family, so to speak, and his legendary reputation, that he justifiably gained in his twenties during his university days, were well-known to most.

His excesses had all come at a cost, as he had just gone through his second divorce, with a further dent in the accumulated wealth that he'd achieved over a short period. Some would say that his choice of wives was not ideal, well, unless you consider an ex-stripper and then an ex-bunny girl that Hugh Hefner had discarded, as suitable marriage material.

Dan and Rico entered the inner confines of the Rivonia management suite, sat down and instantly noticed that a lot more money had been spent on the interior decoration of this room than invested in the rest of the club. Jacko stood up and gave them one of those condescending smiles, the type that you see on a billboard when the local Politician is wanting your vote around election time. He offered his limp hand as a form of greeting and they introduced themselves.

For the first few minutes, they talked about everything but the crimes that had taken place. He then mentioned that he was the owner, which was incorrect as the family trust was the official owner. He also pointed out that, although he oversaw the financial management side of the business, he left all day-to-day operations to his able general manager, James Turner. This suggested to Dan and Rico that he wanted them to believe that he was not responsible for what had happened on that night.

Dan and Rico could smell 'bull-shit' from a mile away and it suggested to them that he was only the general manager of the club, with an attractive monthly salary. He was a middleman who had no real say in the business, as any major decisions were done by the executors of the estate. He left all day-to-day operational 'things' to others, who he recognised were more competent than he would ever be. Like most kids coming from wealthy families, he was another monkey with a degree, completely divorced from reality. He would not be in his present position if not for his parents.

That isn't to say that he didn't have a few million sitting in the bank, left for him by his family. Or that he had been paid annual dividends from the business since the age of ten, as a tax avoidance scheme set-up by the family trust. For someone who just had $1.4 million stolen from his casino yesterday, he didn't appear that concerned.

He then turned to Dan and Rico and said, "Gents, what happen to my money?" with a smile on his face, "have you caught anyone yet?"

Both Dan and Rico smiled back, as it was now only 24 hours since they were first informed about the robbery, the chance of them having nailed someone was highly unlikely. Furthermore, they were surprised at the lack of a mention of the murders that had taken place in one of his guest rooms.

Dan reassured him, "We're working on it around the clock and have our key men on the job. However, we are investigating possibly two crime scenes here and this will, understandably, take-up time."

"Yes, I heard about the two murders. But that was a gay thing, and it looks like a lover's tiff or something, right?"

Rico thought to himself, "So, the fact that they were gay means that their deaths meant nothing?"

Dan said, "We are looking into that and to see if there is a possible link between the two scenes."

"You're saying that there may be a link?" asked Davido.

Dan nodded, "We need to keep all lines of investigation open," and added, "I am sure you appreciate, as part of the investigation process, we need to ask you a few questions."

Jacko nodded and said, "Go ahead."

"Can you please tell me your whereabouts on Sunday night and early Monday morning?"

"I was at the club until around 16.00, then I went into town, had something to eat and went home. I got in and went to sleep at around 22.00, maybe 23.00," he said.

"Can anyone confirm your whereabouts?" said Rico.

"No, as you may have read in the newspapers, I was recently involved in a messy divorce and I now live on my own."

Dan smiled at him, and to make him feel more relaxed, like one of the boys, he said, "Yes, we've all been there, and we've got the badge." he smiled looking at Rico.

Rico thought under his breath, "At least my financial outlays were not as big as his."

"Yes, blood-sucking women, if there was no money in the world, there would be no divorces." It appeared that he was still hurting from his most recent 'play-thing' that had disposed of him, setting themselves up financially for life.

"Can you think of anybody who had a motive to steal $1.4 million, say one of your staff members?" said Dan.

"No, why do you ask?" replied Jacko.

"Well, our present thoughts are that it may have been an inside job."

"Really," he said looking surprised, "I am not sure if any of our staff members would be capable of pulling off something like this. Most of our staff have been with us for years now. We may not be the most perfect employers but, we provide jobs which pay their mortgages." Trying to justify the poor salaries and long hours that his staff had to endure to help him maintain his standard of living.

Dan and Rico had no more questions at that time and excused themselves.

As they walked out of the room, they looked at each other, "What an asshole."

Rico added, "He couldn't manage a non-profit brothel, even if he was giving the sex away for free, he would still screw it up." Both broke down laughing at the thought, and Dan boyishly punched Rico on the shoulder.

It was time for Dan and Rico to interview the key staff.

Chapter 15

Eleanor Birch had been the overnight duty manager on the Sunday night. She was a smart cookie in her early forties and fit for her age, conservatively dressed, and had short cropped hair. She was a strong-minded person who was very confident in her demeanour, perfect for her present position in the hospitality industry. As Dan and Rico don't typically meet ladies like her, they were impressed with her from the start, knowing that she was completely out of their league, that is, if they were ever thinking about taking her out for a drink.

She had been working at the Rivonia for close to five years now and had over ten years' experience in hotel management at various venues. She was recently divorced, had two teenage boys, and was originally from the Philly area.

Being a solid, diligent professional person, she had spent the past 24 hours riddled with anxiety and insecurity about the robbery and the murders that took place on her watch. She had been dreading this interrogation.

Dan started off, "Can you please tell us about your schedule, your duties for the evening of Sunday night?"

She informed them that typically, the duty manager started work around 18.00, and then departed at 07.00 the next morning. Around 22.30, she would meet Andy, the security manager. They would go off to room 212, open-up the inner secure area, and remove the correct money box, the one with Sunday stencilled on the lid. They would then close and lock-down the area before collect the takings.

She would start her rounds, first, she collected the takings from the reception check-in area, then moved on to the casino area, the restaurants and move onto the two bar areas.

Having collected all the takings for the evening, they would then head back to the room 212, where they would re-enter. Once the money box was safely secure in the pen, she would lock up and leave. At all times, Andy, was with her. She would return to the duty managers' office, open the safe, place the keys for room 212 and close the door.

The rest of the evening consisted of doing rounds to make sure the bar areas had been securely isolated, that the cleaners had their instructions for the night, and that the kitchen area was clean and ready for breakfast the next morning. At around one o'clock in the morning, she would have a cup of coffee with the overnight porter, Tony, and leave any instructions with him. She would then review any guest requests for the next morning and finally, go to bed.

There was a small, single bedroom off the duty manager's office where she would have a few hours shut eye, before getting up around 06.00. She would have a chat with Tony to make sure that there weren't any issues overnight, and then she'd make her way to the kitchen to ensure that food-prep was taking place for the coming day. She would have some breakfast, before going back to the office to prepare any hand-over notes. Around 07.00, the other duty manager would arrive to relieve her of her duties. She would then drive home and get her boys ready for school.

Dan said, "Can you please tell me, besides yourself, who else had access to the main safe in the office?"

Eleanor answered, "James Turner, the assistant general manager, and the other duty manager."

"Would the porter have access to the duty manager's office, and to the safe at any time?"

"No," she replied, "He could come and go into the office whenever he wanted, but he didn't have the code for the safe. Only four of us knew the safe code, that I know of." she added.

"What about the latch locks on the money box lids?" asked Rico.

She answered, "The money boxes latch locks had no keys but had digital codes. The empty money boxes were left unlocked, until after the financial controller had finished counting the money for that day. She would then lock the money boxes and no one on site could get access. The boxes were only opened again when safely transported and in the bank."

Dan looked at Rico and said, "That's why they had to use the drill to break the lock latches."

Dan decided to put some pressure on her. "So, Eleanor, $1.4 million has been stolen from Room 212, and two murders took place in room 215, in the early hours of Monday morning. You were the duty manager, so how come you knew nothing about it?"

Eleanor was shocked at the sudden line of questioning, which has started off gently, and was now abrupt and in her face.

"I really, really don't know," she answered, sounding genuinely distressed. "At around 23.30, when I locked the inner gate of the secure area, all the boxes were there, I swear. I have no idea what took place in room 215."

"What time did you go to sleep on Monday morning?"

"After my rounds, I had a cup of coffee with Tony around 01.00, so it must have been 01.30," she said rather nervously.

"At any one time, did you see anything suspicious, did you ever have a look at the CCTV monitor, did you go back past Room 212?" asked Dan.

"No," shaking her head, "Whilst on my rounds, I saw nothing out of the ordinary. Room 212 is nowhere near the main areas, or the duty manager's office, and I had no reason to look in that area again." She said, trying to avoid crying.

"And the CCTV?" barked Dan.

"There is a monitor in the duty manager's office, but it showed nothing of concern."

"How often would you look at the monitor on an average evening then?"

"Well, hardly ever. There's no designated person to monitor the CCTV continuously. We would expect the 'on-duty' night porter, Tony, to monitor it overnight."

Rico then decided it was his turn to come down heavy on Eleanor, "So, let's get this straight, you know that there is a million dollars sitting in room 212, because you transported it there, yet you don't bother to have a look at the CCTV over the course of the whole evening?"

Eleanor said nothing.

"Besides someone stealing $1.4 million dollars, there was a double murder that took place in room 215. Would you know anything about that? It did happen during your shift, after all," he remarked in a sarcastic manner.

Once again, she said, "I am so sorry, but I don't know anything about it and I never saw or heard nothing."

"Did you hear any gunshots?"

She shook her head. "No."

"How long have you known Tony Smith?"

"For roughly two years now." she answered.

"You two were the only ones on site who were staying overnight. Also, you both knew what was in Room 212. How do we know that you both hadn't planned this together? You have the keys for room 212. Between the two of you, you could have pulled it off." said Rico.

Eleanor, was starting to lose her cool and composed demeanour, "Think what you want, but we didn't do it."

Dan then said, "Eleanor, we noticed that your credit score rating is pretty poor. Have you had issues paying off any credit cards, or could you be in financial difficulty?"

She now had regained her composure, and said, "Well, that's what happens when you marry an asshole." she replied. "Like most people, there were times when we experienced financial hardship, especially when you have two children to bring up."

Dan and Rico, suddenly reflected on their own marriage failures, feeling slightly uneasy, perhaps they were just as guilty as the asshole who had come into her life.

She added, just to make them feel more uncomfortable, "My debt is now down to $5k, and is being paid off in an affordable, manageable manner. By the end of the year, my debt should be history.

"Stealing $1.4 million to pay off a $5k debt would be silly, especially if I got caught and I had to spend the rest of my life in jail. I don't believe that my kids would like to visit me in jail."

She had a point, she was smart, they thought. Rico thought of his own personal debt which was now around $25k and rising. Dan's debt was now around $10k, which he would be taking into his retirement in two months-time. Between the two of them, they had just spent close to 60 years working like dogs. Instead of having savings, they instead both had debt that they will still be paying off into their retirement. Their financial illiteracy was legendary, and they could have written a book on their specialist subject.

"I see you're from Philly." said Rico. "Do you know Max Montana?" Both now looked for a reaction from her. It was a long shot, as they knew what the answer would be. No-one as smart as her would be associated with him.

She said "No, I have never met him."

They thanked her for her time and decided to move on.

When she got up and left, they were both thinking along the same lines. They both didn't believe that she had killed the occupants in room 215. There appeared to be no motive, and she was too smart to be connected to a murder scene. She was educated enough to know the consequences. Their general belief was that most murderers were not typically smart people.

"However, she was smart enough to organise the robbery. If she did know Max, and his associates from her time in Philly, then they would have been able to help with the job. Knowing that Tony could have been asleep sometime during the night, she could have entered room 212 and carried out the robbery with someone else, without him picking it up on CCTV." said Dan.

"Or," Rico added, "When leaving room 212, she could have simply left the inner secure door open, then left the entrance door slightly ajar when leaving. So that a third-party, such as an overnight guest, could have walked in at any time to commit the robbery."

Chapter 16

Tony Smith had been working at the Rivonia for close to ten years now. He was sixty-eight years old and had previously worked as an engineer at a nearby factory. However, when the owner decided to transfer the manufacturing section of the business to a location in China, the writing was on the wall for him and many others who worked in the area. Even though he was an excellent, skilled engineer, he could not compete against the low-waged workers in China.

Due to various local and government trade policies, and a mass change to a service driven economy in the USA, engineering was now dead. The local steel mills were relics of the past and for local folk, the American dream was long-gone. However, this perception was still being peddled by politicians who couldn't come up with any of their own original policies to improve inequality and poverty for these hard-working citizens.

Along with his chosen career, his $401k pension that he had saved into for most of his working life was also long gone. It looked like he would be working for the rest of his life. His wife, who he had been married to for over 40 years, had died prematurely from an asbestos related disease, having worked in one of the local mills for most of her life. Most would agree that they were among the thousands of victims left behind by the greed of the billionaires on Wall Street.

He lived on his own in Harrisburg. His only vice, so it seemed, was that he went salsa dancing every Friday night, not that this pasttime was considered a suspicious activity by the local cops in downtown Harrisburg. This all strongly suggested that his lifestyle was certainly not rock and roll, or that they would be signing him up for the next Ocean's Eleven movie production.

Tony came in and sat down opposite Dan and Rico. Despite his age, he looked in better physical shape than most in the club. Like the previous interviews, Dan decided to put some pressure on Tony from the start.

"So, Tony, $1.4 million was stolen from Room 212 in the early hours of Monday morning. Furthermore, two guests were murdered in room 215. You were the overnight porter, tell us about it."

Although Tony had spent most of yesterday thinking about what he would say when they asked him this type of question, he was lost for words and he simply said, "I have no idea what happened."

"What time did you start your shift last night, and what time did you leave this morning?"

"I started at 22.00." he said rather nervously, "and I handed over the reception at 07.00. I then had a quick breakfast in the staff mess, then went home around 07.30."

"At any time, did you see anything suspicious, and what time did you do your rounds?" asked Dan.

"I did my rounds at 02.00 and 04.00, and I never saw nothing suspicious. I did walk past Room 212 and 215, but I saw or heard nothing."

"And the CCTV?" said Dan, "did you ever look at the CCTV monitor? How often would you look at the monitor on an average shift?"

Tony quickly realised that he was responsible for monitoring what happened at the club overnight and he had to be careful what he said, "Yes, over the course of the morning, I would constantly look at the monitors, but I saw nothing."

"So, besides someone stealing $1.4 million dollars, there was a double murder that took place in room 215. You know nothing about it, even though you happened to be on duty."

Tony nodded.

"Would you ever fall asleep, whilst on duty, intentionally or not?"

He said "No, besides doing my rounds, I have enough to do most evenings." He then pointed to his pedometer watch on his wrist, and it showed that he had walked 22,000 steps in the last 24-hour period, hoping that this would prove his innocence.

"How long have you known Eleanor?"

"For two years now."

"As you two were the only staff members that stayed overnight, how do we know that you both hadn't planned this together?" said Rico.

Tony once again shock his head, "Sorry, we didn't do it."

Chapter 17

The security at the Rivonia was overseen by two security managers who addressed any issues that may take place in the club.

Most of their work involved dealing with confrontational customers being aggrieved by their perceived, self-inflicted, misfortune. Customers who frequented these casinos typically walked in with an inflated ego, their self-confidence on a high. However, in most cases, this soon dissipated once reality kicked in, they'd lost their hard-earned money. Fuelled by excessive alcohol and guilt, the inevitable confrontation could become hostile and abusive.

Both carried a gun, which was on constant show for anyone who was thinking about vandalising the slot machines or harassing a courier. There were two twelve-hour shifts, starting at 06.00 in the morning and finishing at 24.00. Overnight, there were no security guards on site. On the Sunday night, Andy the security manager had been on duty.

Andy Johns was the Rivonia head security manager, and he had held this position for close to ten years now. Obviously smarter, as well as physically larger than the other manager, he was the one chosen to head-up security. He was unhappily married, possibly due to the fact he was constantly broke. He had two demanding teenager daughters who were expensive and regularly in trouble.

He was ex-military, having served in the Iraq war, which suggested that he knew how to use his gun. The average drunk, hostile patron would be no match for him. Having found an opportunity to discharge himself from the army, he landed up at the Rivonia, a natural career progression for most ex-military men.

Having had the 'crap' kicked out of him, and his enlarged ego deflated during his initial army training, he was now a good, honest member of the local community with solid moral and social standards.

When Andy walked into the room, Dan and Rico, took one look at him and decided he was a man to be respected. Standing around 6 ft 3 inches tall, they didn't want to get on the wrong side of him, nor try and cuff him if he got aggressive. Although they were both crime-busting veterans, they knew their limits, especially when dealing with younger, larger men with a forceful nature.

Having introduced themselves, they began to discuss the crimes that took place while he was on duty Sunday night.

"We were told that around 23.00, you and Eleanor drop off the money box at room 212. Did you go into the room at the time?"

"No," said Andy, and added, "Whoever is on duty, they always stand outside the bedroom door, whilst the duty manager locks up the takings for the night. When the duty manager is inside, the entrance door is always shut. The routine is there to protect the door, in case anyone decided to overpower the duty manager and steal the money during this time."

He added, "I am sure CCTV would show this fact." Dan and Rico had already confirmed this.

"Have you ever been inside room 212?" asked Rico.

Andy confirmed, "Yes, on a few occasions. I have been asked to assist when the CCTV was broken, or if I wanted to review a section of recording. Once, I helped move a money box that had been jammed when it lost a wheel. I entered the area only when instructed by the duty manager."

"The issue we have here, is that you were on duty on Sunday. A few hours later, $1.4 million was stolen from Room 212, and two guests were murdered in room 215. You are also head of security for the club. Have you any idea how this all took place?" asked Dan.

Andy sat there thinking about it, "I've spent the past 24 hours thinking why, or how, someone could have broken into the space. Having seen the lay-out in the room, I strongly believe that it must have been an inside job that took place after 24.00. If that is the case, I can't be held responsible for what happened as I was at home."

"What time did you leave the club?" asked Rico.

Andy replied, "I left the club around 23.30."

"Can you think of anyone who would have a motive, say, a member of staff?" Added Rico.

"Well," he said with confidence, "with regards to the robbery, the motive was $1.4 million. The question is who had the opportunity to pull it off? With the shootings, it looks like a separate event which may have been motivated by jealousy. I can't think of any staff member who would carry out those crimes."

He added, "I think that it could have been a hotel guest who was fed information from a staff member."

Dan and Rico nodded, and it was good to see that someone else had the same opinion they had about how the crimes had been committed.

"Can someone confirm that you were tucked up in bed, in your own home, between 24.00 and 06.00?" asked Rico.

"Yes." he said. "But I didn't go straight to sleep, as I was waiting up for my two daughters to come back from a party. But there were at least three people who could confirm my movements after 24.00."

"This robbery that took place looks like a well-planned and executed job, perhaps requiring military-type discipline and precision. Have we any reason to suspect you?" said Rico. Dan was relieved that he was not the one who asked the question.

"No, said Andy, "I give you my word. I didn't do this, even if I did have the opportunity." he added, and they believed him.

"Have you ever worked in Philly or Baltimore?"

"No." he said

Dan and Rico came to the same conclusion that his moral compass was pointing in the right direction, a highly disciplined human-being who always kept on the right-side of the law. Although he was probably once a ruthless mass murderer when he was running around in Iraq, most would agree that he had a justifiable reason for his actions.

Chapter 18

James Turner was the general manager, a role that he had only recently taken on. He was in his late twenties, a slim man, well-educated and articulate. After three years at the Harrisburg College of further education, he had a diploma in Hospitality management. This was his first position and he was keen to impress.

He sat down at the table fearfully as, although he wasn't at the club at the time, they may want to link him to the crime in Room 215.

"James, can you please describe your movements on the Sunday?" Asked Dan.

He told them, "I worked for most of the day and then around 16.00, I took the rest of the day off. By late Sunday afternoon, the club starts getting less busy, so I took the opportunity to have some time off. I returned at 07.00, on the Monday morning."

"Can someone confirm your movements?" said Dan.

He answered, "Not really, as I live on my own."

"Where do you live?" said Dan.

"In Harrisburg." he replied.

"Do you have any idea who may have carried out the robbery?" said Dan.

He shook his head, "I have no idea."

"When was the last time you were in Room 212?" asked Dan.

"On Sunday morning when I let Lisa into the room." he replied.

"Whilst in the room, did you notice anything out of the ordinary, such as the money boxes having been forced open?" asked Dan.

"No, it all looked in place." He replied.

Rico probed further, "You are the general manager of the club, you knew what was contained in Room 212 and you had access to the keys. Not only that, you had the afternoon and evening off, which means you could have re-entered the club and carried out the robbery. Should we consider you a possible suspect?"

James shook his head, "No, no, I'd never do something like this. I've only been in this role for the past six months. I would not do anything to compromise my position."

Rico added, "The gents who were murdered in room 215 appeared to be gay. Did you know them?"

"No." he said.

Rico then added, "But you are gay?"

He looked slightly nervous and then said hesitantly, "Yes." but added, "I'd never seen them before, and I had no reason to kill them."

Dan and Rico then dismissed James.

Dan turned to Rico and said, "How did you know he was gay?"

"I can just tell." said Rico. Dan raised one eyebrow, looked at him and said, "Go-on, tell us how's that then."

Rather than coming out with a major revelation, Rico just said, "Eleanor told me." They both had a good laugh.

Dan said, "Well, if he was off for most of Sunday night, he had the time to carry out the crimes. However, to do the robbery, he would need to enter the duty manager's office and remove the keys from the safe without anyone seeing him."

Rico added, "He may not be involved in the robbery, however, perhaps he killed the two who were murdered as they were gay."

They realised that they were speculating again, with no clear evidence to support their theories. Furthermore, he had only recently been employed at the club, so they did not suspect him of these crimes.

With that, the financial controller arrived at their table for the next interview.

Chapter 19

Lisa Brew had been working at the Rivonia now for eight months. She had recently married for the second time. She was in her forties, a fit, bubbly person, with shoulder length, blond hair and seemed to be a dedicated member of staff.

Most mornings she arrived at the Rivonia around 07.00, after having some breakfast in the staff canteen, she would then arrange the money floats for the day for the various bars and restaurants. Once these were delivered, she would head back to the office and make coffee. She would find the duty manager, who would then retrieve the keys for room 212 from the safe.

Around 09.00 each morning they would both enter room 212, the duty manager would open the inner secure area and leave it open. She would be locked in the office for the next two or three hours, or however long it took to count the money. Once the money had been counted and the bank pay-in slip completed, she would secure the money box lid within the internal secure door.

The entrance door to room 212 was self-closing. She could exit, but if she wanted to get back in, she would need to get hold of the duty manager.

Once the counting was complete, she would change the previous night's CCTV cassette for another tape, so that the coming evenings activities were recorded. She would then notify the duty manager that she had finished, reassuring her that she had not stolen the overnight takings, that is, if she wanted to. The rest of the day was made up of general administration duties.

Dan and Rico beckoned for her to have a seat.

As before, Dan started off. "Lisa, $1.4 million was stolen from Room 212 in the early hours of Monday morning. As you worked in the room most days, can you please tell us what you know?"

"I had no idea that the robbery had taken place." she responded.

"Can you tell us when you were last in room 212?"

She said, "On Sunday morning between 09.00 and 11.30, when I counted the takings for the previous evening."

"Was it a typical day? When you were in the area, did you notice anything out of the ordinary?"

She replied, "Everything was normal, there was just me in the room."

"Were the boxes still intact, had the latch locks been tampered with?" asked Rico.

"No, they had not been tampered with." She replied.

"Who else had been in the room, say in the last few weeks?" said Dan.

She responded, "The duty managers would sometimes bring in a cup of coffee and join me for a chat. Andy, the security manager had been in, once or twice, when there was an issue, or I needed a hand with something. The owner, Mr Jackson, occasionally came into the room, to discuss general and financial issues."

"How would Jacko enter the room?" asked Dan.

This questioned took her by surprise, but she answered, "He would gently tap on the door, and then I would let him in."

"Have you ever seen him use his own leys to enter the room?"

"No." she said.

"Has he got the key for the inner secure area?"

"Yes." she replied, "However, I've never seen him use the keys to enter the area. When he has come in, the inner door had always been open."

"You change the CCTV cassettes over every day?" asked Ricco,

She nodded.

"Is anyone else familiar with the procedure?"

"Well, yes. Andy has, on occasions, asked me to give him a recording if he wanted to review an incident that may have happened overnight. The duty-manager knows how to change over the cassettes. Jacko and James would also have a good idea how to operate the machine."

"Do you have any debt, Lisa?" asked Rico.

She responded, with a smile on her face, "Well, I recently got married for the second time, so we have had an expensive few month." Then added, feeling guilty and needing to justify her expenditure, "Like I am sure most newly-weds would have in the same situation. I'm sure it will be paid off in the next few months."

"We were looking at your husband's bank records. Do you know that he has $50k in debt?"

She attempted a smile, "Yes, I am aware of that." She had not been aware of this fact until last week when she came across his monthly bank statement, which she still needed to discuss with him sometime.

"We are looking for a motive for someone stealing the $1.4 million. If you stole the money it would have paid off all yours, and your husband's debts. You knew the money was there, did you steal the money, Lisa?" asked Dan, wanting to see her reaction on her face.

She responded, "I would never do anything like that. I'm sure my parents would confirm that I am a good Catholic girl educated in a convent. I swear on my mother's life that I did not do this."

Lisa then left. Dan turned to Rico and said, "So, what you think?"

"I'd like to bang her," said Rico, then laughing, "sorry, are you asking if I think she did it?"

"You were brought up in a sewer." said Dan, laughing.

Rico gave it some thought, "She knew the money was there and she was in the area for two to three hours, that's enough time for someone to drill out the rivets and empty the money into their bags.

"As she managed the changing of the tapes, she could have made sure that the recordings that we saw were from the previous Sunday night, seven days earlier. Furthermore, no-one went in after her, so they can't confirm whether the money was still there."

"That's what I was thinking, she had motive and opportunity." said Dan. "Although, she did say she was a good Catholic girl."

Rico said sarcastically, "My ex was one, and there was nothing pure about her. She showed no mercy when it came to the divorce."

"I still think Jacko may have done it." said Dan. "Knowing the daily routines, having let himself in, he had the chance to spend the whole afternoon in there. He could have then changed the CCTV recordings."

Chapter 20

Back at the Harrisburg bureau, later in the afternoon, a quick briefing took place before interviewing Mad Max again.

The results had come back from the lab, and Natalie confirmed the contents of the mobile phone, highlighting a text that Max had received at 07.30. Dan read the text out loud:

"Job went to plan, expected arrival at Motel, 09.00, Franco"

Dan and the team discussed the message in detail. "When he refers to the 'job' was it the robbery or the murders? The word 'job' could mean both." They all contemplated.

"Does it matter?" said Rico, "if we can pin just one of the crimes on him, this will improve our chances of putting him away."

The cell number was registered in the name of Mr Franco Martello, at an address in a working-class suburb in Philly, which was now being investigated by the local police department. Max also came from the Philly area. There appeared to be regular telephone contact between them, suggesting that there was some connection between them before these crimes took place.

Dan, said, "So, it seems that this gent, Franco Martello, who sent the message, is an associate of Mad Max. The text links them to the job and both were located near the scene of the crimes."

They all just realised that this was the first positive break-through in the case, which was good news.

"Any other info?" said Dan.

Harry said, "It appears that Max was a frequent visitor to Regina's in Philly. Some saw him at the club on numerous occasions. However, none would confirm if he were 'batting for the other side' or not, out of fear of the man's reputation."

"Could Mad Max have paid someone to bump off an ex-lover? But how does this connect with the Rivonia robbery?" said Dan, searching for an additional possible motive. No one could come up with a suitable explanation for a link.

Harry added that he had interviewed the Gardens motel staff who were on duty last Sunday night and they confirmed that Mad Max had checked in at around 22.00 on Sunday evening. They never saw or heard of him again until he blasted one of their bedroom doors full of bullets.

They were given access to the motel CCTV. However, it only covered the reception area and some parts of the main car park. The motel was of an 'L' shaped construction. Room 104 was situated around the corner, not in direct line of the car park camera, so they never picked up any movements. There was also a small car park in this area which also wasn't on the camera's line of vision.

No one had any further information to add. Dan then reminded everyone that they still had nothing, and they needed to find who the other two gentlemen were. If Franco Martello was the shooter, they needed to find him fast.

Dan turned to Irene, "Can you please do some digging and get some background on Mr Peter 'Jacko' Jackson, if he has a gambling habit or not, how much debt he may have? With all this free time he has now, he may find solace at a local casino.

"Also, can you investigate Eleanor's past? She was from the Philly area and who knows, she may know Franco Martello, or Victor Stanley."

Chapter 21

Mad Max was escorted into the interview room, Dan and Rico came in after him.

"You sleep well?" said Dan to Max.

He replied, "Better than my previous night in the motel." He smiled at them.

"You received a text yesterday morning at 07.30," said Dan, "Who was the text from?"

Max's mouth became dry in an instant. They had accessed his cell phone and knew the contents.

Max did not reply.

"Perhaps the name Franco Martello may mean something to you?" asked Dan.

Max certainly knew the name but decided not to answer.

"Your records show that you have been in contact with him over fifty times in the past six months, five times in the past week. This suggests that you knew him, and that you knew what was taking place at the Rivonia."

Once again, Max said nothing.

"Who is Victor Stanley?" Max also knew who he was but wasn't going to volunteer any further information that could incriminate him. How he wished that he had never met Victor, as he would not presently be sitting here.

"Who is the third person, you must have a name?" Max was not saying anything.

Dan was getting frustrated and said to Max. "Perhaps another one of your gay buddies from Regina's?"

Mad Max looked at Dan with a smile and said, "Perhaps."

"Max, two people have been murdered and $1.4 million has been stolen from the Rivonia. The text on your phone confirms that you and Franco knew about what took place. Then there's the fact that you fired four shots at our police officers, attempting to kill them. You're going down for a very long time." said Dan.

"Why don't you tell us what happened?"

Mad Max said nothing. He knew that the evidence was stacking up against him. Getting out of these charges was going to be a challenge.

As they were walking out, Rico turned to Dan and said, "It would be easier asking Donald Trump not to lie at one of his daily briefings, than to get any information out of Mad Max." This caused them both to have a good laugh.

Chapter 22

The local Philly cops arrived at Franco's apartment, knocked on the door and gave a loud verbal warning. As there was no reply, they got the locksmith to open the door.

Once inside, there was no sign of Franco and everything appeared to be in place. Besides what some may consider an unhealthy selection of porn videos, there was nothing that suggested he was a ruthless killer. The neighbours confirmed that they hadn't seen him for a few days now.

The local Philly police knew of him, as anybody associated with Mad Max were generally up to no good and would eventually come onto the police radar. For most people with half a brain, the link is indisputable, so one couldn't think of a logical reason why they would want to become friends with him in the first place.

Franco had a tough upbringing as he was another child from a fatherless family. He was certainly not further-education material and, having finished high school, he tried his hand at various non-crime related jobs. However, he never lasted long in these jobs. This was possibly due to an underlying issue that he always had when being given simple instructions. He had a large chip on his shoulder and any instructions were perceived to be an unacceptable order, no one told him what to do. He then progressed to a life of crime where he came across Max, his adopted mentor.

He was of slim-build, so jobs that he may have been attracted to, such as working as door-security at a nightclub, weren't an option for him as he did not have any physical presence. Rumour had it that he was Mad Max's driver, go-fetch man and he was always eager to please his master. Once given a gun, he suddenly had a reputation, and this inflated his previously non-existent self-worth. Recently, there had been a few unsolved murders in the local area. Rumour suggested that Franco, under the instruction of Max, had used his gun more than once.

He was generally regarded as a small-time player wanting to be a big-time player but did not have the know-how to improve his reputation. For some reason, he thought that hanging about with someone called Mad Max would improve his street cred. The local police were familiar with Franco and they'd had the opportunity to arrest him on two occasions. However, the charges could never stick, as the victims and witnesses failed to go through with the accusations. Through excessive intimidation, their original statements would be retracted, to the constant frustration of the local law enforcement.

His ex-girlfriend was initially reluctant to divulge any information about him out of fear. However, once told that he was up for murder, she was happy to share more than most, hoping that he would go to jail and she would never see him again. In the first stages of their relationship, he appeared okay, but then things got worse. He turned into a sadistic psychopath and she was terrified of him.

Having once found a gun in the house, she confronted him, and he responded by giving her a beating she would remember for the rest of her life. The beating included him pulling the gun on her, putting it to her head, and threatening to kill her. This whole nightmare had gone on for three hours and had put her off all men for life.

The only photo they had was from a driver's licence on a national database. It was an old, unclear photo, taken when he was seventeen and had a beard. The fact that his girlfriend had no photographs of him suggested that even she wasn't keen to be seen in public with him.

The photo that they had of him did not appear to match the pictures they had of the two victims discovered in Room 215, although they had no way of matching eye colours, which presented a definite challenge.

Chapter 23

It was another early start on the Wednesday morning. Once again, everyone was congregated in the briefing room, each with a cup of coffee in their hands, gorging on Irene's donuts that she brought in. Having read the psychological profile they received from the Philly cops, they all concluded that Franco needed to address some obvious mental and behavioural disorders that he must have. It suggested that he would have killed the two victims in the bedroom without a second thought.

The possible scenario was that he was a paid 'hit-man' and had been instructed by Max to 'bump off' both victims, perhaps on behalf of someone else. There may have been another motive, such as jealousy or resentment, however, as both were lying in the morgue, they couldn't verify this.

The local cops in Philly set-up a surveillance team across the street from his apartment, and it was monitored continuously. Franco's motor car was finally tracked down to the Gardens motel car park, which linked him to the crime scenes. It also suggested that he had driven Max down to the Gardens motel, as he had no means of transport. Max then dropped him off later, Sunday night, at the Rivonia, as Franco was spending the night there. This arrangement ensured that Franco's car couldn't be placed at the Rivonia, the scene of the crime on the night.

In the morning, when leaving the motel, Franco could have used one of the victim's cars, as he now had their keys. Having arrived back at the motel, he saw the police bust-in taking place. He then decided that it was perhaps not the most suitable time to meet up with Max, so he then decided to drive on and disappear. His car at the Gardens motel provided Dan and his team with a definite link between the two men and the crime.

"If we had arrived at the motel fifteen minutes later, the outcome of this case would have been very different." said Dan. Unfortunately, when they needed divine help from above, it never worked in their favour.

All the CCTV recordings covering the local interstate road were reviewed but they did not pick up the exit route that Franco may have taken. It was a mystery where Franco was, and it appeared that he had just disappeared into thin air.

"Any other information?" said Dan.

Harry replied, "My man down at the Riverside Casino in Harrisburg, confirmed that

Jacko is a Platinum member, an exclusive member of the club and he was a regular there. Rumour has it that he'd had a few big losses there recently, but no one would verify this.

"We have no idea what his financial losses are at the Casino, and if would be difficult to get hold of this info. However, perhaps he didn't want his parents or his staff, to know of his gambling habit. Or if the gambling laws allowed him to gamble in his own casino."

Irene came in, "Besides the two very expensive divorce settlements, around $5 million in total, this suggests that he may have had few outstanding debts that he doesn't want us or anyone else to know about."

"He appears to have limited luck when it comes to women and gambling. A complete loser, in more ways than one." added Rico.

Harry then said, "Furthermore, he was at the casino on Sunday afternoon, arriving at 16.00 and leaving around 22.00, which is not what he originally told us."

"That's interesting," said Rico, surmising, "He had the spare keys for the doors in room 212, he knew of the coming and goings of the staff, perhaps he came up with a plan to get rid of his debt?"

It was time to visit Jacko again, so they set off for the Rivonia once more.

Chapter 24

They arrived at the Rivonia, headed towards the management suite, and entered Jacko's office around 11.00 am. He offered them a cup of tea, but they declined as they had more important things to discuss with him.

"So, gents, what's the latest then?" said Jacko.

"We are working on several lines of enquiry and we are still at the early stages." Dan said to help reassure him that they were still on top of the case.

Dan started, "Regards the last visit we had, when asked what you were doing on Sunday night you were, some would say, economical with the truth. Would you like to tell us what you were doing on Sunday evening?"

Jacko squinted and looked at both with disdain, pretended to think about it, and then said, "As I told you before I was at the Riverside Casino, where I had something to eat and then went home."

Dan looked at Rico, "Do you remember Jacko saying he was at the Riverside casino?" Rico pulled a face suggesting that this was news to him.

"No, Jacko. You did not mention the Riverside casino. Furthermore, we believe you arrived there around 16.00 and left at 23.00, which is not what you told us."

Jacko decided that the best form of defence was to attack, "Sorry, your line of questions suggest that you think I am the main suspect in this enquiry." He looked at them in an accusing, searching manner.

Dan, smiled, knowing that Jacko had been rattled, "Not at all, Jacko, its standard investigation procedure. We need to eliminate the good guys first."

Jacko lightened up, and said, "I do apologise, I should have been more specific about my whereabouts."

"We believe that you are a platinum member, suggesting that you are a regular client of theirs, is this correct?"

Hesitantly he said, "Yes, I am, so what does that have to do with the enquiry?" once again he looked aggrieved at the line of questioning.

"Well," Dan tried to explain, "If someone were carrying a serious amount of debt, and that person happened to own a casino, this would suggest a possible motive."

Jacko said angrily. "That is ridiculous."

Dan then added, "Do you have any personal debts?"

Jacko was now furious. "I am not sure where you got this information, but it is incorrect. My line of credit extends to half a million dollars with the Riverside casino, which can be easily paid-off at any time."

They had obviously stirred-up the man's ego and as they had no intention of falling out with him, they excused themselves and left the room.

"What you think?" said Dan to Rico.

"This all depends on how much he had sitting in his bank." he smiled. "If there is still $10 million, well, why would he rob his own casino? Also, I am sure the bank of 'mommy and daddy' would help him out if necessary." said Rico.

Rico reflected on his own life, and said, "Unfortunately for me, when I was eighteen, my dad gave me with a packet of Lucky Strikes, a bag of condoms, and told me to piss-off."

Chapter 25

Sunday night at the Rivonia was typically the quietest night of the week. During the week, the club had a constant clientele of businessmen, choosing to stay at the Rivonia rather than in Harrisburg. They had various meeting and function rooms, and companies who were keen to spoil their staff could book them into a nice country-located club, which also has a casino and a golf course. At the weekends, they had many out-of-state golfers and gamblers who would stay over, taking advantage of the facilities that they had to offer.

On Sunday night, there were only twelve guest bedrooms booked out, of which there were twenty guests for the evening. Only four guests had previously stayed in the club, suggesting that most of the guests were not familiar with the layout of the club and what room 212 contained.

One group consisted of fourteen men who were attending a conference in one of the club's meeting rooms the following day. They had spent the day playing golf, had an evening meal and some fun at the casino. Most of them were in bed by 23.00, having had too much to drink, which suggested that they did not require further questioning. Only one guest had come from the Philly area, but was quickly dismissed as she was elderly.

The remaining guests were contacted and interviewed, however most confirmed that they were there only for the facilities. Stealing the casino takings, or carrying out a murder, wasn't on their agenda for the evening.

However, one male guest caught their attention, as it appeared that he had no reason for being at the motel, as he didn't play golf or spend much time in the casino. He had booked a single room, which suggested that he was on his own.

The whereabouts of Mr Brian Williams in room 120 was not known. He had, like Franco, just disappeared and they were trying to track him down. Could he be the person who may have helped a member of staff carry out the robbery on the Sunday evening?

Chapter 26

It was Thursday morning, and they all were in the briefing room expecting Dan to appear. Irene had prepared the coffee for all and another box of Dunkin Donuts waited for them. The eating of donuts every morning was now part of their staple diet, providing all the essential carbohydrates that they didn't need for the day.

Dan walked in, picked up a donut, and said to Irene, "You know, if you carry on feeding Rico these donuts, he will never find another wife." The room broke into laughter at Rico's expense.

Dan started, "Right, what do we have, make my day."

Irene informed them, "Eleanor, whilst at College, had worked at several bars in and around the Philly area, however, there are no suggestions that she knew Max or Franco. Tony Smith is squeaky clean, a model citizen, with no-known criminal offences."

She told them that Andy, the security manager, was known by local cops as a teenager. It appeared that his parents may have lacked the necessary parenting skills to keep him in check. He had a record for petty theft, fighting, and a few other minor offences, typically related to drugs, however, he had been let-off. His parents sent him off to the army, hoping he would become someone else's responsibility and would self-correct along the way.

This appears to have worked and suggested that being regularly shot at by Muslim extremists was a form of behaviour correction therapy, for any parent thinking that their son had lost their way.

Natalie King from forensics, drifted in, and reported her latest findings. "Nothing came back on the blood types, the dental records, or the hair samples. The bullets used for the murders were from a Beretta Model 70 and there is evidence that a suppressor, or silencer, may have been used. This suggests that it could be a 'hit-job'.

"The time of death was between ten to twelve hours before the bodies were found, so they likely died around 23.00 and 01.00 on Sunday evening, or Monday morning, which is consistent with the single gentleman entering room 215." She had no further information to add.

As they still could not recognise who the person leaving was the next morning from the CCTV recordings, they were nowhere near finding the killer, so they moved onto the robbery.

Various scenarios were discussed, and one was that, as Jacko may be in financial trouble, having to pay off his debts, he had decided to rob his own casino. He was the only one with both sets of spare keys to room 212, and he may have come back to the club instead of going home to sleep on Sunday, as he had said. He could have avoided passing through the club reception, so that no one would recognise him. Once the job was complete, he then changed the CCTV recordings for the previous week.

He had the keys for the inner and outer doors, but he didn't have the codes for the latch locks on the lids, so he would have had to drill out the rivets holding the latches.

Rico pointed out, "However, we are assuming that he had the necessary technical skills to operate the drill. I would be surprised if he knew how to hold the portable drill that was used, never mind trying to find the switch to operate the thing."

Dan smiled at how Rico described the scenario.

Dan then said, "Looking at everyone who worked at the club, only a few people would have known how to operate the drill that drilled out the rivets holding the money box lids. On that Monday morning, whoever had the keys to open the secure door, either Eleanor or Jacko, they must have got someone to drill out the latches on the money box lids. That was either Tony, who was on duty at the time, who was previously an engineer, or Andy the security manager."

Harry added, "Or an overnight guest at the club."

Natalie then said, "Excuse me," and everyone turned around to look at her, "As there is nothing on the CCTV recordings for the period, why are we assuming that the robbery took place between 24.00 and 06.00 on Monday morning? This robbery may have taken place the previous afternoon, after Lisa had left the room."

Dan looked at Rico, and the others. She had raised a good point, even though they didn't want to admit it, "Yes, you are right, it could have happened before the Sunday evening, good point." looking at Natalie to acknowledge her contribution.

Those in the room were shocked to have just experienced the parting of Natalie's lips, suggesting a smug smile. It was one of those, "I was there when it happened" moments. With that, she got up and left the room as she had other important things to do.

In an instant, they were having to rethink the whole crime scene. Could the robbery had taken place earlier, in the day or evening? Could someone had been hiding in the bathroom area, so when Eleanor came in, she never looked in the area and left? Or she knew someone was there all the time. Or did Lisa leave someone in the room in the morning?

As the security guard never came into the room at 23.00, he wouldn't have detected the empty money boxes. Then if the CCTV cassette had been changed before the person left the room, the recordings would have shown no improper activities.

If this was the scenario, then the murder scene has nothing to do with the robbery.

This line of investigations was getting them nowhere. So, they decided to widen the scope of the investigation.

Dan asked Irene, "Have you contacted the Rivonia to find out who repairs the A/C ventilation systems at the club? Also, who has the CCTV maintenance contract?"

Having got the contact details for the A/C man, Irene had typed his name into the national crime database, which brought up his details. He had a business called Johnson's Plumbing & Electrical services, based in Harrisburg, specialising in air-conditioning, plumbing and electrical repairs and installation.

In his early twenties, Greg Johnson had done three years at Frackville Correctional Institution for vehicular manslaughter, where he was involved in a hit and run and had left the scene.

Could this be the break in the case that they had been waiting for? It was well worth visiting him, they all thought.

Chapter 27

They jumped into the car and drove off to the other side of Harrisburg, across the Susquehanna river. The address led them to a small industrial estate, consisting of several small domestic garage-sized units. All occupied by genuine, small businesses trying to make an honest living.

They came across Unit 12 and pulled into a vacant parking spot. Outside was a pick-up truck with a sign on the side displaying 'Johnson's Plumbing & Electrical Services'. They knew that they were in the right place.

They got out of the car and entered the unit where they came across the occupier, sat behind his office desk and on the phone. He beckoned them to sit down opposite him and signalled that he would be two minutes before the call was over.

Greg Johnson appeared to be in his early thirties, he had a beard and scraggly hair and was dressed in old, well-worn, dirty overalls. The contents of his workshop consisted of old pipes, valves, bottles of gas, compressors, and electrical boxes, all typical for someone offering his range of services.

He put down the receiver, and with a big smile, introduced himself, "Gentlemen, what can I do for you?"

Dan and Rico introduced themselves, then briefly outlined why they were there and that they were interviewing all contractors who had worked at the Rivonia in the past.

Dan started, "Have you read about the Rivonia casino break-in?"

Greg Johnson was calm and said, "I haven't read about it in the papers, as I am dyslexic," smiling at his misfortune, "However, I saw something on the local TV news."

"As you've worked there in the past, can you tell us what your work involved?" Asked Dan.

Greg, pointing to the contents in the unit, said, "Gents, as you can see, I am a pipe, valve and re-gas man. I do anything that involves water and gas. I have, in the past, done a few jobs at the Rivonia, some were reactive jobs, such as fixing water leaks. I have also serviced their A/C plant, which needs constant care as is now old and needs replacing. I also replaced all the water taps in their guest rooms around a year ago."

Dan and Rico observed that he came across as a friendly type of person, constantly having a smile on his face, and he looked like a genuinely nice guy. Someone who you would have a drink with at the end of the day.

After 40 years of investigating hundreds of different people, they both were a good judge of character and the simple test they had was, would they have a drink with that person? In most cases, if the answer was no, that person was a possible suspect and would likely end up being arrested.

"When were you last at the Rivonia?" said Rico.

Looking in his diary, he replied, "I was there on the 2nd November when I re-gassed a cylinder for them."

"Before that." added Rico.

Greg replied, "Around a year ago now. I was asked to replace around 100 taps in the guest room's toilets for push-button types."

He then related the story that due to water shortages in the county, they had decided to install push-button tapes in all the toilet areas. The fact that there was no restriction in water usage on the golf course irrigation made the whole thing a joke. They all smiled at the irony.

"Did you have to access the ceiling void areas?"

"Yes," said Greg, "The isolation valves for each water supply to the guest rooms were above the entrance door. I had to lower the access door hatches, so the valves could be isolated before I did the repair."

"Did you ever have to climb into the main ceiling areas, in the corridor areas, and walk around?"

Once again, answering with a smile, "No, I had no reason to climb into the loft space. What I remember is that in most cases, it would be a real challenge, as the access areas above the hatch doors was limited for anyone wanting to crawl around the ceiling space." Dan nodded, having seen the space for himself.

"Have you ever had access to the main ceiling space, say when you were servicing the main A/C plant?" said Rico.

"No, the work that I did on the A/C plant was all external. I changed the fresh air inlet filters and re-gassed the compressor, which are located outside, near the kitchen area."

He added, "Besides the main ventilation ducting, I don't believe there are any other mechanical plants, such as fans or pumps in the ceiling void and therefore, I had no reason to enter the space."

"Did you ever enter the safe secure room area?"

Greg looked genuinely confused, "What safe secure room are you talking about?"

"One of the bedrooms had been converted into a secure area to store the casino takings." said Dan.

Greg looked surprised and said, "I don't believe that I've ever seen this room and couldn't tell you where it is. I am sure that if I had been in the room, I'd have known."

"Do you do ventilation ducting?" said Rico.

Greg said "No, gents," twisting his body around and pointing around the unit, "As you can see, I'm just a pipe, valve and re-gas man." Dan looked around the workshop and he did not see any evidence that suggested that Greg maintained or installed ventilation ducting.

Rico then said, "We noticed that you did time at Frackville. What was that all about, then?"

The blood drained from Greg's face, and he said, "Guys, I am sure you saw the details of the case, I was nineteen years old at the time. It wasn't a premeditated crime, and the judge saw it that way as well. Running-over a drunk homeless man, unintentionally, is one thing. It doesn't mean that I now walk around carrying firearms, shooting people, or planning casino heists." He added to justify his innocence, "I wouldn't even know which way to point a gun.

"You surely can't pin what happened at the Rivonia with what I did twelve years ago now?"

Dan nodded his head and said "Yes, you're right."

"However," said Rico "You linked the murders with the casino heist. How did you know they were linked?"

Greg suddenly realised they had put him on the spot, "Well, it was the way the TV news reported it. If you ask anyone in the street, I'll bet that 90% will say that the two events are linked."

Dan and Rico's questions were getting them nowhere and it was time to leave. Greg walked them over to the car, they shook hands and said their goodbyes. Just as Dan was pulling out of the car park, he called out to Greg, "Do you do car A/C re-gassing?" He smiled and gave him a thumbs up.

Turning out of the driveway, Dan turned to Rico and said, "So, what do you think?"

Rico thought about it for a moment and said, "He seems to be a genuine person, and his smiling, empathic character suggests that he could not have killed someone. Well, compared to Franco, the psychopath, he comes across as a pussycat. What happened twelve years ago suggests that he was in the wrong place at the wrong time."

"Yes, you are right, however, could he have planned and executed the secure room robbery?"

"No, I don't think so. The last time, he spent any length of time at the Rivonia, was over a year ago. Also, if you had $1.4 million sitting in your trunk, would you still be working in that shitty workshop? Anyway, he's a pipe, valve and re-gas man." said Rico, causing them both to chuckle.

After a few minutes of driving, Dan turned to Rico and said, "That hasn't solved our problem of how the Rivonia secure room was broken into."

It had to be an inside job carried out by a staff member, they both thought.

Chapter 28

The Harrisburg Commercial Security Systems company was well known to the local cops, as most crimes that took place in the area had their CCTV monitoring equipment on site. They were a well-established, family-run company, having offered their services to the local area for over 30 years now. Their offices were situated alongside the Susquehanna River, overlooking the city island, and the connecting bridges.

Sitting in the owner's offices, they had a general discussion about the CCTV systems that were in place at the Rivonia. They had been informed about the non-functional camera in the public car park, and at the next scheduled service, it was going to be addressed. It had not been repaired earlier, as the owners hadn't wanted to pay the 'call-out' fee.

Over the years, several different technicians had serviced the equipment, however according the maintenance contract that was in place, this was only an annual visit, which suggested that they were never on site long enough to plan something like the robbery that had just taken place. Furthermore, they would not have known anything about the comings and goings of the staff into the area.

Also, as pointed out by the owner, due to the nature of their business, they were automatically linked to every crime that took place in the area. It wasn't worth the risk to their reputation to be involved with any form of crime and Dan fully understood.

He was just about to leave, when he asked Bob, the manager, "If you were wanting to enter the safe secure room, and you didn't want to be detected by your CCTV systems, how would you do it??"

"Well, CCTV monitoring does have its limitations," he replied, "If the operator chooses to not change the tape each day and just tapes over the previous day, then any records are erased and gone. Or, if someone alters the day of the week by changing the name of the day stuck on each cassette, then the recordings become meaningless. The recordings are only as good as the management system in place, which is open to abuse if in the wrong hands.

"You could, also," he added, "take a picture of the CCTV monitor recording in the area, get it printed, and then climb up a ladder and somehow stick it onto the front of the camera. This will create a fake view on the monitor. I've never seen it been done before, but I have seen it done on various murder mysteries on TV." He smiled.

Dan and Rico thanked him and left. When in the car, Dan turned to Rico, "Are you thinking what I am, that the tapes could have been tampered with, or an image of the corridor placed in front of the CCTV camera lens? With this picture in place, the suspects maybe opened the entrance door of room 212, stole the money, left the room and then later removed the image."

Rico looked at Dan, nodded, and said "I was just thinking the same, this must be an inside-job."

They went back to the Rivonia, sourced a stepladder from Alan, climbed up and had a closer inspection of the camera covering room 212. There appeared to be no evidence that the camera had been tampered with.

Whilst there, they re-interviewed Eleanor and Lisa, but came up with nothing of importance, or that could give them a lead. They headed back to the bureau.

Chapter 29

By Friday, Dan and his team were getting frustrated at the lack of progress. Dan banged the briefing board and said, "Gents, we have nothing," and everyone looking at the briefing board agreed with him.

Under the casino robbery heading on the left side of the board, the only possible suspects that had were all members of staff, as they still believed that it was an inside job. This list included: Jacko, Eleanor, Andy, James, and Lisa. They all had a clear motive, the $1.4 million sitting in room 212, and they all had various opportunities to execute the robbery. The issue was that they had no hard evidence to suggest that any of them had done it.

The possible third parties who could have carried out the robbery, the A/C and CCTV contractors may have had the technical knowledge to execute the crime, however, they may have not known what was in room 212. Also, they had no idea of the routines of the staff, or when the money arrived and exited the area.

They all knew, unfortunately, they were nowhere nearer solving the crime and that speculation as a source of motive didn't count in the court of law.

Under the murder crime scene section on the right-hand side of the board, the evidence seemed clearer. They believed that it was a professional 'hit-job' organised by Max and executed by Franco. The crime scene had been cleaned and it looked too clinical to suggest that a member of staff had done it. Furthermore, the motive for killing the two men did not fit their profiles and suggested that there was no link with the staff members.

"The only thing we have," added Dan, "is a message linking Mad Max, and Franco, to the Rivonia job. As this would not be the first time he has been linked to a murder or a robbery, there's a good possibility he had something to do with it."

It was starting to look like two perfect crimes had taken place, both executed at the same location and time, within ten metres of each other. The only good, positive news was that Mad Max was finally to be charged for accessory to murder, culpable homicide, obstruction of justice and attempted murder for trying to kill a few cops.

Chapter 30

Five weeks had passed, and they had re-interviewed everyone that was associated with the crimes at the Rivonia. They reviewed all the forensics again. They had also widened their investigation, to include other external contractors and known cons in the area who may have carried out the job. They had nothing that could have given them the break-through they needed.

The bottom line was that there were still two bodies sitting in the morgue, and as they had no eyeballs or fingers, it was a challenge to identify them. They all agreed that if they had some form of positive identification, they would have something to work on.

They also had no idea if both cases were linked, or how they got in and out of the room 212, the safe secure room.

They all concluded that the murders in Room 215 were a 'hit-job' and they were dealing with an experienced professional, as he had left no traces of evidence and the executions were clinical. It appeared that Mad Max had arranged the hit and it had been carried out by Franco, perhaps on the behalf of a third-party.

They still had no idea who Victor Stanley, or the third person was. Even though there was a nation-wide appeal to help find Franco, and he was on the most wanted list of the CIA and FBI, he had not surfaced at all in the past few weeks. The local police department in Philly had eventually shut down all further surveillance operations.

Eleanor and Tony were still arriving at work every day, suggesting that they didn't have the money. If they had, they would have been long gone. Typically, most first-time cons who suddenly come into money, go out and squander the proceeds on things like fancy motor cars and other luxuries. There was no evidence of that having taken place.

The Rivonia security guards showed no indication of being involved in the robbery, and they were still coming to work every day, suggesting that they were also in the clear.

They had carried out secret surveillance at all their houses for the past few weeks, and besides one or two male acquaintances that visited Eleanor's house, there was no suggestion that she and Tony were more than work colleagues.

There appeared to be a regular visitor, of dubious character, to Andy's house, suggesting that he or his two daughters had a cannabis habit that would not go away.

James appeared to have finally found true love in Harrisburg, and a young man was regularly staying overnight.

When Jacko's bank details were finally confirmed, it showed he was down to his last $4 million, suggesting that he did not have to rob his own casino.

The good news was that Mad Max would soon experience what the inside of a courthouse looked like, as for most of his life he had managed to avoid the pleasure. Most police departments in the local counties were happy to hear of his capture, however most would agree that it was at least thirty years too late.

Dan and Rico could live with the glory that they were the ones who finally put Mad Max Montana behind bars for good.

The solving of the Rivonia crimes was going nowhere, and as other crimes needed solving, the time and effort of key staff were reallocated. It appeared that whoever committed the Rivonia crimes had simply disappeared and the crimes would never be solved.

As Dan was due to retire the following week, he met with his superior officer for a final debrief. They went through any pending cases and tied-up any loose ends that needed addressing. Dan did offer to stay on so that they could crack the Rivonia case, but everyone knew that any further progress would require Mad Max to squeal, and most knew that he would take the information that they needed to his grave.

In Dan's forty-three-year career, he had cracked most cases that he worked on, and his record was exceptional. He was disappointed, as he would have liked to have nailed the last one, the Rivonia crimes, but this was not to be.

However, as he was reminded by his colleagues, he had more successes than losses and with a success record like his, he shouldn't lose too much sleep on the last one, or two, that had gotten away over the years.

He also realised, that he was not thirty years younger, and didn't have the same motivation that he once had. His youthful ego and drive were now gone, and it meant that he did not feel the need to stay and finish the job. It was time to retire and play golf with some fishing in between.

Chapter 31

Dan's retirement party came and went, and he had been retired for two years now. He had settled down to enjoy his retirement, which consisted of either fishing or golfing on most days. Boredom and predictability were a regular feature in his life, which he had to accept, there was nothing else on offer. He still couldn't afford a girlfriend, so he chose the company of a bottle of gin, which he replaced every other day.

Out of all the cases that he'd cracked, there was still one that woke him up during the night. He would regularly re-think and go through all the facts of the Rivonia case. Occasionally when playing golf at the Rivonia, he would walk past rooms 212 and 215 and wonder if he had missed something.

On one of the hottest days of the year in Harrisburg, the air-conditioning in his Buick, which was now close to twenty years old, had finally packed up. He decided that it was now time to give his car A/C system a well needed re-charge of gas.

He looked up the contact details of the local A/C gas recharge centre and pointed his car in the direction of the address. When turning down a road he realised that he was driving past the unit where Johnson's Plumbing & Electrical Services was located.

Remembering that Greg Johnson was an A/C gas-recharge man, he decided to turn off and entered the business unit complex. He stopped outside unit 12 but to his surprise, the unit was shut and there was a 'For Rent' sign on the door.

Dan found a nearby space, parked the car, and then wandered off across to the fast-food outlet located on the opposite side of unit 12, to buy a burger and a soft drink. Whilst waiting, knowing that the burger vendor would know everything that went on in the road, he asked him how long the 'For-rent' sign, at unit 12 had been there for. The burger-man replied that it had been empty for at least two years.

Having paid for his items, he then sourced a bench under a tree and sat down to consume his lunch. While he sat there, he wondered where Greg Johnson could be.

He picked up the mobile phone and gave Irene a call. "How are you, gorgeous? When are you going to find a real man and leave that husband of yours?" In an instant she knew who it was and after a few moments of catching up, along with some outrageous flirting, he asked her to do him a favour.

She took down the name of Greg Johnson, his last known address, and she said she would phone him back in 10 minutes. She entered his details into the local business and citizen contact databases that they used, which showed no recent addresses. She then used the national licence database, which showed no recent offences. Having no luck, she then searched on the nation-wide government databases, including the FBI and CIA, but still no luck.

After fifteen minutes, Dan received a call came back from Irene. It appears that Mr Greg Johnson had simply disappeared and there was no trace of him anywhere. They said their good-byes and promised that they would go out for a drink sometime.

Dan was surprised to find that Greg had suddenly disappeared. Could Greg be the person who masterminded the whole operation? There was no way that such a large amount of money could have been moved like that, not without some help. Perhaps as he couldn't do the job himself, he needed help, so he contacted Mad Max.

Could the two 'no-eyes and no-fingers' victims, be the thugs that Mad Max organised to help him do the job?

With both dead, Greg would then have access to Franco's cell phone, and he could have been the person who sent the text to Max. He always felt that the text did not 'feel' right as if it was written by a third-party, written for someone else and not for Mad Max. Was he the person who contacted the police bureau and spoke to Irene? The more he thought about it, the more it started to make sense.

The only way the money could have been stolen is via the ceiling space somehow. He was the only person who had any experience of the ventilation systems and the building layout. He had done time in prison, suggesting that he had the contacts to source the help that he needed to facilitate the robbery or to get hold of a gun.

Could he be Victor Stanley and was the elusive Franco Martello one of the victims that lay in the morgue for over a year? Had he used his own car, and this was this the reason why they couldn't trace the suspects' exit the following morning?

The past two years of Dan's life had been boring and predictable. However, within minutes, the adrenaline was kicking in again and for the first time since his retirement, he was feeling alive, like a wolf seeking the blood of another suspect.

However, there was nothing he could do about it. He was retired, the case had been long closed. Due to state budget cuts, the department had been re-integrated into another. Furthermore, the key staff had all moved on or retired. Due to these recent moves, Rico had decided to move states and he had become an independent private investigator. He must have hoped that he could conveniently hide his monthly income without his exes and children knowing. Once he had saved some money then he could, perhaps, remarry.

Even if he walked into the bureau tomorrow, and said, "Hey everyone, I've finally solved the mystery of the Rivonia job." Would anyone be bothered as no-one was familiar with the crime, besides knowing that it was never solved by those working on the case at the time?

Furthermore, Greg appeared to have disappeared into thin air, perhaps to the same place that Franco would have been, sitting on a beach bar in Florida somewhere. He knew that most crimes became meaningless if they couldn't find the suspect and they soon became a distant memory.

Retribution Man

Chapter 32

Greg Johnson was born and raised in downtown Greenberg, outside Pittsburgh. His father took one look at young Greg, decided that childcare was not his 'thing' and was long gone. His mother was a single parent who worked long days to make sure they had a meal on the table and that her only son ended up with a decent level of education at the end of it.

However, things never went to plan, as they discovered Greg had dyslexia. He was always at the bottom of the class when it came to educational achievements. Being aware of his disabilities, he kept a low profile at school, however when he was at home, he was a restless kid, constantly out and about looking for the next adventure. He was certainly not going onto further education.

After high school, he joined a local plumbing company specialising in providing Air-Conditioning services to the commercial and domestic sectors. After three years he gave up on trying to pass any of his national vocational certificates as they were written exams, which he struggled with. However, he was an excellent technician, better than most, especially when it came to the repair of anything that was mechanical or electrical. He could also install and maintain large-scale commercial ventilation systems, which he did regularly.

One night, Greg met up with some friends for a few drinks at the Barroso's cocktail bar and grill. He heard some shouting taking place behind him and turned around to find a young couple, in their early twenties, having a domestic argument. Within seconds, the drunk boyfriend punched his lady in the face and while she was still reeling from the impact, he kneed her in the groin.

Greg, having experienced this injustice, jumped off his chair and forced himself between the two, attempting to stop the fight. The two men argued, which cascaded into the drunk guy swinging at Greg, his fist impacting the side of his face. As they were in close quarters, Greg shoved him fiercely, so he fell backward, slipping on the way, before cracking his head on the side of the pool table. In an instant, blood poured out of the back of his head and quickly covered the surrounding floor.

Greg, in sheer panic at his unmoving victim, and thinking that he had killed him, ran out of the bar and got into his truck. Reversing out of the car park, he sped off, wanting to get as far away as he could. He had not gone a few minutes when he approached some traffic lights. He slowed down, but as they changed, he accelerated again. Unknown to him, a homeless drunk had staggered onto the intersection, and Greg's truck hit him at 30 miles-an-hour. The drunk 'man-with-no-name' was killed on impact.

He pulled over and stopped the truck. He urgently got out and ran around the back, to discover one dead homeless man. His heart stopped, and for the second time that night, panic hit him like a sledgehammer, he jumped back into his truck and sped off. "Oh Jesus, what have I done. My life will never be the same again." he thought.

He parked the truck down by a local river and spent hours wrestling with his thoughts. He had just killed not one, but two people. He was going to jail for a very long time. He called his mom at around 03.00 am crying his eyes out and explained what he had done. She strongly advised him to not go on the run as they would soon find him. She reminded him that she had not brought him up to kill people and what had happened was not entirely his fault.

The next morning, after a sleepless night, he handed himself in to the local Greenberg police bureau.

The court case, a few months later, was a horrible experience for the whole Johnson family. The drunk man in the bar did recover from his injuries and was never seen again. The judge did take into consideration that Greg had no previous record and that the unfortunate death of the nameless homeless man was a vehicular homicide with no planned intent. However, as he had fled both scenes, the judge showed little pity, and he was jailed for three years at Frackville Correctional Institution.

Jail time for Greg was harsh and it was a sharp learning curve for real life. It was an alternative life of hardship, a world full of undesirables, misfits, narks, and psychos, who were keen to use or abuse the weak or vulnerable. The first few weeks for Greg were brutal, as jail was no place for his smiling, empathetic nature, and there was a queue of cons who wanted to take advantage of him.

The saying is that when you must fight you have two options, 'fight or flight'. Unfortunately, in jail there is nowhere to run. It was more like 'fight to survive', there were no other options. He hardened up fast and came to recognise who the narks and the psychos were, and who to avoid. He also learned to be constantly on his guard, as scenarios changed in an instant, and his long-term well-being could be quickly compromised.

He kept a low profile during this time. However, as he could fix most mechanical or electric things, with time he became the man to go to if you wanted something repaired, which the inmates constantly took advantage of. As he was of some use to them, he was left alone for the remainder of his jail term.

When the ventilation or the water systems broke down in the prison, he would help fix the issue. He soon became the unofficial maintenance man, which was recognised by the governor, but Greg was never remunerated for his services.

Three years later, he came out of jail a different man, now having a degree in self-preservation and as streetwise as any other con who had just left Frackville.

Chapter 33

When he was released, he returned to Greenberg and the security and fine comforts of the family home. He approached his old company to see if they would offer him his old job back, but the company had gone into administration. These were desperate times for him as he found it difficult to get work anywhere. He couldn't shake off the three years missing from his employment record.

He knew he was good at what he did and all he needed was some luck. He also knew that he had to get out of Greenberg, with its small-town mentality. He would always be remembered for that one thing; he ran over and killed a homeless man. The only solution was to leave Greenberg and leave his past behind him.

He loaded-up whatever belongings and tools that he had into his truck. He said goodbye to his mom, who understood his predicament and set off for Harrisburg, or any other town that would accept him.

Arriving in Harrisburg, he found a place to rent and soon sourced a unit for his new business. To avoid having to mention his past prison record, he knew that he had to operate and manage his own company. He registered a company called Johnson's Plumbing &

Electrical Services and purchased some advertising space in the local Yellow Pages. He was soon in business and all he needed was some commercial clients.

With time, business picked up and Greg was soon making good money. As, in most cases, he did all the work himself, he was generally cheaper than the more well-established firms in the area. Furthermore, as the business offered a range of mechanical, as well as electrical services, once he got his foot through the front door, he was in constant demand.

Having received a call-out from the Rivonia Golf Club and Casino, he arrived on-site and found the assistant general manager, who pointed out the plumbing issue that they had. Within hours, the issue was solved, and all were happy. Over the next two years, his services were in demand at the Rivonia, and he soon became familiar with the layout of the mechanical and electrical devices.

He had the opportunity to provide a quote for the replacement of all the taps in the guest bathrooms, which was awarded to him. He had to change over 100 taps and it meant spending three weeks on the job.

The job entailed removing the existing taps and replace with new, push-button type taps in all the guest room and public areas. It involved first opening the ceiling hatch door directly above the bedroom door entrance, which contained the incoming cold and hot water supplies and isolation valves. When these main supply valves were shut-off, he could then replace the taps in the bathroom area. Once the pressure was back in the system, he would then test to make sure there were no leaks and then move on to the next room.

This job took place around twelve months before the Rivonia crimes.

Chapter 34

Whilst at the club replacing the taps, Greg arrived at room 212 and saw that it was not a standard key card entrance, so he went off to find the duty manager. When they both arrived at the room, the duty manager took out some heavy-duty keys, which did not look like standard door keys and entered the room. Before he went in, he was informed that this was the safe secure room, where all the money takings from the club and casino were stored before removal from site to a high-street bank in town.

When he entered, he saw Clare Meek, the financial assistant who was counting the money from the previous night's takings. He noted that the section where the money boxes were stored had a steel wire mesh partition wall, and the door had a heavy-duty locking system, which would have been a challenge for most professional thieves.

He was then informed that while Clare was in the room, and if he did not help himself to any of the takings, he could carry out the replacement of taps in the bathroom, which was only used by her.

When it came to isolate the main incoming water supplies, he had a problem, as the ceiling access door was not there. It had been removed when the room was been converted into a safe secure room. Furthermore, the ceiling of the room had been fitted with fire retardant sheet panels. In case a fire broke out in the club, it would not extend into the safe secure area and burn the money, which was a sensible idea, he thought.

He notified Clare that he had to go back into the common corridor area to source a ceiling access hatch opening so that he could find the incoming water supplies. He then found an access ceiling hatch not far from room 212. Having secured his ladder, he opened the access door and with the help of his flash torch, he looked inside the ceiling void.

To his surprise, it was large enough for a man to stand upright in due to the club building having an A-framed design. He then lifted himself into the ceiling void and explored the space.

The space was open-planned and dark. He noticed that the area contained numerous ventilation ducting systems, hot and cold-water pipes, with electrical cables scattered everywhere. The main ventilation ducting for the club ran the length of the ceiling void and there were individual ducting take-offs for each bedroom. To avoid stepping on the ceiling, as it may collapse through to the corridor area, he balanced his weight between the horizontal joists that supported the roof. Having sourced the water supplies for room 212, he isolated the valves and headed back to the ceiling hatch door.

He proceeded to exit the space, by retracing the steps where he had entered. With a small tap on the entrance door to room 212, Clare let him back into the room so that he could complete the tap replacement.

Once back in the room, he was soon flirting with Clare. She enjoyed the fact that she had company and a younger man was paying her some attention. With time, she told him that the money was delivered by the duty manager and security guard at around 23.00 every night, where it was left for the night. Every morning at 09.00, she was allowed entrance into the room to count the previous evening takings, which she then bundled ready for the transport.

Once a week, on a Monday morning, Fidelity Armed Transit Services would pick up the money boxes and transport them to the bank in Harrisburg. When asked how much was in the money boxes, Clare said that she could not say, but smiled and suggested that it was a lot.

They carried on chatting and he discovered that she was soon leaving the Rivonia as she was moving out of the state.

Before leaving the room, he looked up at the ceiling and noticed that the main ventilation supply for the bedroom area was in the secure pen area and that it was a simple plastic grille that could be easily removed. He quickly scanned the room and noticed that there was no internal alarm system that one would expect. "They were only relying on the heavy-duty steel mesh partitioning wall to keep their money safe," he thought.

Before leaving, he informed Clare that he was about to pressurise that system again and that if there were any leaks, she should come running out and tell him. He then re-entered the ceiling void in the common corridor again and opened the main hot and cold supply taps to the room. While in the area, he had a good look around. Within minutes, he had a plan on how he could rob the Rivonia safe secure area of its contents, the casino takings.

At the end of his working day, before heading back home, he proceeded to one of the bars at the Rivonia and had a drink, His head was spinning. Could he really break into the safe secure area and steal the money? It must be more complicated than his simple plan. The next question was, just how much money was in those boxes?

He finished his drink and went into the casino area. He always thought the gambling past-time was a silly idea. One worked hard all week, then give most of it away to a rigged machine. He couldn't see the logic in the pointless past-time played by people with inflated egos.

He counted thirty slot machines and by the weekend these machines would be working overtime. Add the three roulette wheels, the bar and restaurant takings, this would add up to a significant amount. Doing a rough calculation, he worked out that if the average person blew $100 every hour, including drinks and food, this came to roughly $10,000 an hour.

Multiplying the hours and the days of the week, this came out to around $1 million, at least. "Phew," he thought, "no wonder the transportable money boxes were so big."

He drove away from the club, thinking that there was possibly $1 million in those boxes, and he was the only person in the world who had a good idea how to access room 212.

There were several concerns that he needed to consider. For instance, there were CCTV cameras constantly monitoring the area and he couldn't put a ladder up in the middle of the corridor without anyone noticing. It would take time to remove the ducting, to get into the area, and to remove all that money. Furthermore, it would take at least two or three men to re-locate the $1 million from the area.

Over the next few days, his practically minded brain came up with a brilliant plan that was simple to execute. He made good use of the rest of his time working at the Rivonia, where he then started to implement his plan and secure his access into the secure safe room.

The main issue that he had was that he would have to rely on others to help him. As most of his school friends were not recognised cons, he'd have to get help from elsewhere, and he knew exactly where to find it.

Chapter 35

The drive up the Interstate 81 took him around an hour. On the outskirts of Frackville sat the maximum-security correction facility, where Greg had wasted three years of his life. Consisting of a group of characterless buildings, surrounded by high razor-wired fence, it was never going to be a must-see building whilst you were in Frackville, that is, if you ever wanted to visit the place.

When he left Frackville State Correction Institute, he vowed that he would never return to the place again. However, there he was, checking into the visitor centre, being patted over by the screws. Two of them recognised him, making sarcastic remarks about his return. He was visiting his old friend, his adopted mentor, who he had shared a cell with for most of his time there.

The entrance consisted of one long corridor which took him from the visitor reception into the centre of the prison, it was a short journey from the previously secure paradise into the epicentre of brutal insanity. The prison was typical of most, overcrowded with noisy inmates and the constant harassment from the prison guards looking for an opportunity to make your stay more unbearable. Some, given the chance, enjoyed the pleasure of inflicting various forms of physical punishment, or mental torture, on the inmates. Any possible reform of character was unachievable, as the system was designed to dehumanise the inmates and was run by incompetent, ego-driven maniacs. The main intellectual activity to prevent the ever-lasting boredom was working in the main laundry, which was only a luxury for the select few.

Greg gave his old friend, Jon Smythe, a big hug, and he was grateful that he had visited him, as he hadn't had any visitors for some time now. He was in his late sixties, overweight, and counting down his time. A career criminal who had been in-and-out of prison more times than he wished to remember. Some said that he had a rap sheet longer than the list of hookers that Donald Trump had allegedly paid off.

After a short chat about prison life in general, Greg informed him why he was there and what his latest 'get-rich' scheme was. He didn't go into too much detail as Jon did not know of the Rivonia.

He wanted two men to help him carry out the robbery. The men had to be experienced cons, not local, and clean if possible. Jon nodded his head, confirming that this request would not be an issue. Greg smiled, not believing that Jon knew anyone who wasn't a con.

The main criteria were that they had to be slim-in-build as they had to fit through a 3ft by 2ft rectangular opening.

"Should they come with a gun?" said Jon.

"No," he said, "it's not necessary." He smiled again, thinking that the only people that Jon knew would always carry a gun.

"What's the job worth?" asked Jon.

Greg took a deep breath and said, "Around $1 million."

"Phew," said Jon, "I wish I were out of here, I'm sure I could have helped you."

Greg took one look at his rotund stomach, pointed at his belly, and said, "I don't think so." They both had a good laugh.

Jon knew of a 'fixer', a man who could help source the right people for the job. He informed him that it would come at a price, and he gave him some solid advice. The man was a 'hard-core' thug who nobody wanted to fall out with. He should always watch his back and limit the details of the job, otherwise the fixer would cut him out and do it himself.

Jon also informed him that if it all went to plan, and to protect his recent financial gains, it would be a good idea to get himself a gun. He needed a shoot-first, ask questions later policy.

Greg had a good understanding of the new world that he was about to step into and that it was not going to be joyride. However, he also knew that he couldn't do this job alone and had to rely on undesirable human-beings, career thugs with guns.

His experience gained doing time in Frackville was soon to become a valuable education.

Within a few days, Greg was given the contact name of the 'fixer'. His reputation was legendary in the Philly and Baltimore areas, and his name would be associated with most major crimes within these areas. His name was Max Montana, commonly known as Mad Max.

Chapter 36

Greg and Max agreed to meet at an out-of-town hotel on the Interstate 81, half-way between Harrisburg and Philly. Arriving in the car park on a cold, windy day they were glad to find a quiet, warm area of the lounge where they could cement their recently required friendship, one out of necessity, not one that would be long-term.

The initial meeting with the man called Mad Max was frightening, to say the least. Greg knew all too well that in the criminal world, reputation meant everything. Meeting someone called Mad Max meant that he did not necessarily have to go into the fine details about his past, nor did he need to see his Curriculum Vitae as proof of his previous activities.

For a moment, he wanted to dump the whole idea and get out of the lobby as fast as he could. But one does not arrange a meeting with Mad Max to then change their mind, unless they wanted a bullet in the back of the head and their body left in the car park.

After some short introductions, Greg soon realised that Max had limited interest in small talk or pleasantries, so he got straight to the plan. He emphasised that no planning for the robbery was required on Max's part, as it had all been previously organised. The access to the secure area was already in place, and all that was required was for Max's two-helpers to pitch-up, take his instructions and help him with the money.

Max was to book two rooms at the Gardens motel on the outskirts of Harrisburg, one for him, the other room for the other two gents. Although the other two had no intention of sleeping there, as they were to sleep overnight at the Rivonia.

On Sunday night, they were to wait at the Gardens motel and around 22.00, would receive a text from Greg. Max would then give them a lift to the Rivonia and drop them off at the public car park. The two gents would then enter the club and order a drink at the bar, where he would meet them. The robbery of the Rivonia casino safe secure would then take place.

In the morning, to avoid suspicion, they would all leave the club separately, then meet up in the public car park where they would drive back to the Gardens motel. At the motel, the money would be split in half, and they would go their separate ways.

The robbery was to be done his way, with his instructions, or he would call off the job. Max could see that he was serious about his threat and his attempts to gain more information from him were in vain.

For Max, who was already in retirement, but always willing to listen to the latest job offers or potential opportunities, this job sounded too good to be true. He didn't have to organise a thing, well, besides finding two skinny thugs who would do his dirty work for him. His reward, once he had wasted Greg, would be being able to walk away with close to $1 million. "What could go wrong?" he thought.

Max agreed with the basic terms and they shook hands on the deal. In an instant, Greg released that he had just shaken hands with the devil and had ventured over to the dark side. One-way-or-another, it was going to end up in tears. That is, if he didn't keep his wits about him.

Max made a quick call and a short time later; two thin gentlemen entered the hotel lounge. They had previously been sitting in the car park, waiting for his instructions. Most in the room wouldn't have automatically identified them as obvious cons, but Greg saw them coming from a mile away. Although they appeared pleasant enough, they were obvious career thugs and he instinctively didn't trust them from the start.

His time in Frackville had made him aware that friendship meant nothing and that nobody could be trusted. All cons, given the opportunity, would 'screw you' over. He had no intention of being friends with them and there was only one important criterion that he was looking for. That was, to satisfy the job description that was on offer, they had to be able to fit into a 3ft by 2ft access space, which both looked like they had qualified.

He met his new associates, Franco and Roberto, and only first names were given, which he believed were not their real names. There were no handshakes or small talk that took place. He introduced himself as Victor Stanley and they briefly went through the plan again, highlighting the fact that all they needed to do was pitch-up and help him remove $1 million.

Franco, in his early thirties, was long and lean and had hips like a racing snake. His name and his dark-tanned-looks implied that his parents may have originated from somewhere in the Mediterranean. Some local members of the opposite sex may have considered this desirable, however, his cold, heartless character, would soon put an end to any longing to get to know him better.

Roberto was in his late thirties, short in size and stature, an ex-jockey. He came with a severe limp, suggesting that his last fall from a racehorse was his final ride. He had 'rat' type features with a chiselled chin and a pointy nose, causing an instant dislike for him. It was obvious that they were both products of a challenging childhood, where love and security were not readily on offer.

As Max did all their talking for them, neither said much. Greg also noted that they didn't like to smile, as this could be a sign of weakness, a possible flaw in the tough character they were trying to personify.

Franco and Roberto were relieved to know that no detailed thinking was involved, which was always a challenge for them, and only their physical attributes were being called upon. Whatever outstanding reservations about the plan that they may have had was easily overcome with the thought that there was $1 million at stake. They all finally shook hands, climbed into their cars, and drove off in different directions, Greg heading back down the Interstate 81.

Victor, alias Greg Johnson, had a sudden panic attack and asked himself, "What the hell have I just done?"

Chapter 37

Two weeks later, the day that was agreed when the heist was to take place, Greg loaded up his Ford SUV with his overnight luggage and set off for the Rivonia, arriving around 14.00 on Sunday afternoon. Instead of parking in the hotel car park, he parked in the public one. He sourced a nearby luggage trolley, loaded it up and headed towards the reception.

Once at the reception, he confirmed his name and room number. Room 215 had been previously booked under the fictitious name of Victor Stanley. He was given two key-cards for his door and he then went to his room. He took advantage of the offer from the bellhop to push the luggage trolley to his room, then tipped him before he left.

He went into room 215, a bedroom that he had previously spent some time in, so was familiar with the layout. As he had previously requested, there was one double bed and one single bed in the room.

Having dropped off his luggage, he decided to leave the room and have a stroll around the club and explore the facilities. It was a busy period, with the casinos and restaurants working overtime. To ensure he was not recognised, he had grown a beard and a moustache, and he wore a fake pair of glasses. He arrived at the lounge bar and sourced a table in the corner. He ordered a soft drink and a sandwich and then spent his time watching the various activities taking place.

Around four o'clock, having finished his meal, he went back to his bedroom. He went through his plan for the last time; however, everything had been planned previously and was put-in-place twelve months ago now. Knowing that he had gone through the same routine at least a hundred times now in his mind, it was time to execute.

He spent the next few hours reading a book and eventually had a small sleep, knowing that he had a long night ahead. Later, during the evening, he went back down into the bar area and had a drink and something to eat, whilst observing all staff movements.

Around 22.00, he sent a text to Max, and as instructed, Franco and Roberto arrived at the Rivonia bar at around 22.30. They sat at the bar and ordered a drink. Greg, noticing that they had arrived, went up to the bar to order another drink, and slipped them the spare card key for room 215.

Fifteen minutes later, they both left the bar, found room 215 and used their key card to enter the room. They noticed that, besides the beds, and the trolley containing three suitcases and a hanging suit cover, there was nothing else to suggest that they were about to steal $1 million. The two of them looked at each other and started to wonder if this was a scam and they had been duped. They then made themselves comfortable and waited for Greg to enter.

Greg stayed in the bar area until 23.00. He saw the duty manageress and the security manager arriving in the bar area with the transportable money box. It appeared that their money collection routine had not changed in the past twelve months. A short time later, Greg finished his drink and left the bar and headed to room 215. With a gentle knock on the door, he opened the bedroom door with his key card and went in.

Franco was the first to jump up and confront him accusingly, "So tell me, what the hell is going on here, what's this job about, where's the gear for the job?"

Greg was calm and looked at the two for a minute and said, "As I told you before everything is in place. I'm poking the cat here, you're just holding the tail, okay?" He added, "If you want to do this job, just listen to me, and do what you're told. If you don't want to trust me, then there's the door, you can leave any-time."

Greg then took the first suitcase off the luggage trolley, put it on the bed, and opened it to remove the contents. He pulled out three all-in-one-lightweight cotton overalls and some plastic shoe sole covers. He also took out three pairs of medical rubber gloves and surgical skull caps.

As instructed, they removed their clothing, then put on the overalls and the shoe covers that they were given. Whilst removing their clothes, Greg noticed that both had guns strapped to their bodies, which made him immediately uncomfortable. "Oh, great." he said under his breath.

Pointing towards their guns, Greg made his thoughts clear, "Where we are going, we don't need guns, okay?" To reassure them, he added, "When we get back into the room, you can have your guns back."

They reluctantly agreed, even though Franco suddenly felt extremely insecure, as his gun was a security blanket to him that he wore at all times.

With their overalls and sole covers on, they then put on the medical rubber gloves and pulled the skull caps over their heads. Greg explained that this was all being done to make sure that no traces of evidence would be left behind at the scene. This is, if they hadn't worked this out themselves. He then instructed them to switch off their cell phones and to put them into the bag with their clothes and guns.

The two thugs were coming to realise that Greg was a professional, and had a disciplined approach to carrying out robberies, not the free-range method that they were familiar with. Usually, their break-ins involved beating up security guards, breaking glass windows, then having to leave the scene in a rush as they had set off the alarm and finally being shot-at by chasing cop-cars.

He sat down with them and explained the access procedure, which was repeated at least three times. The operation was to be carried out in total silence, and the only means of communication was through hand signals and nodding of their heads.

Around 23.30, Greg went to the bedroom door and slightly opened it, so he could see and hear the money box been delivered into room 212. Eventually, he heard the noise of the money box been transported and the two staff members talking. A few minutes later, they closed the door of room 212 and the duty manager said, "Thanks Andy, and good night."

Around thirty minutes later, Greg repositioned the bedroom chair directly below the ceiling access hatch and climbed up. With the help of a screwdriver, he undid the four screws that held the lid in place and once removed, the hatch door fell-down on its hinges. Leaning through the hatch, he grabbed a stepladder, one that he had left there twelve months ago. He guided the stepladder through the hatch and positioned it on the floor.

Greg then climbed up the ladder and pulled through an electrical extension cable, which was then plugged into the bedroom wall socket. In an instant, the ceiling area above the hatch lit-up. He lifted himself through the hatch and instructed them to follow him. Franco and Roberto were amazed at what they saw and climbed up the step-ladder into the ceiling void.

Besides the ladder, he had purchased six long 6ft by 2ft rectangular ply-wood boards, which he had placed horizontally across the supporting horizontal roof joists. This would make crossing the ceiling space easier, ensuring that none of them slipped and fell through the ceiling. This would also be a big help when bringing the money bags back into the bedroom.

They followed Greg along the length of the ceiling space until they got to room 212. Above room 212, there were four bags waiting, one containing some tools, the other three were collapsible luggage bags for the money that they were about to steal. Removing two spanners, he proceeded to remove the eight nuts and bolts that were screwed to the main ventilation ducting, which was attached to the discharge grille in the room.

Once the bolts and nuts were removed, he signalled for them to get on each side of the ducting and to lift the section off its joints. It lifted easily enough, and they gently placed the section of ventilation ducting to the side, making sure it was resting between two joists for support.

Greg then removed the ceiling grille with ease, which he then placed to one-side. Looking down through the rectangular-shaped hole, they saw the seven money boxes, each one with the day of week stencilled on the lid. They passed the ladder that they'd used to climb into the ceiling space between them and placed it into the rectangular ceiling opening. Once the ladder had a firm grounding on the floor below, Greg climbed down into the safe secure area.

Under his breath, he said, "That's stage one complete, three stages to go." He then signalled to Franco to pass down the bag with the tools. The other two then climbed down into the space, each smiling as they suddenly realised what was at stake.

Greg then took out the portable electric drill from the bag and proceeded to drill out the rivets holding the heavy-duty latch locks on the lids. Within minutes, he had drilled through one, and then the next two. He inserted the sharp edge of a crowbar between the latch and the lid surface and with a yank, the latch popped off. "One lock down, six to go." he thought.

Having broken the lock latch, Greg lifted the lid to find the whole box was filled with bundled dollar notes. He looked at the others, their eyes transfixed, gorging on the contents like a child who had just received the keys to a candy shop.

On top of the stacks of money bundles in the money box was a note, a bank remittance slip that had been prepared previously. The slip showed that the contents of the box contained $201,750. Greg pointed to the slip and then pointed to the other money boxes, in sequence. If all the boxes contained similar amounts, this would roughly come out to $1.4 million. They all looked at each other and nodded at this information.

Whilst Greg was drilling out the latches from the other boxes, the other two were transferring the money into the collapsible bags. Two hours later, the time approaching 02.30, the job was complete, all $1.4 million had been removed. They left the same way they had entered, but this time in reverse and with the four bags full of money.

Once out of the safe secure area and in the ceiling space, they replaced the grille, fitted the section of ventilation ducting back in place and then fixed the bolts. Once complete, they left everything as it had been. Shuffling along the boards, with the bags in tow, they finally arrived back at room 215 ceiling access opening. Franco and Roberto, with the help of the stepladder, dropped back down into the bedroom space. They dropped the bags of money in the bedroom.

Greg then lifted the ply-wood boards and twisted them 90 degrees, between the vertical joists, laying them flat on the ceiling, so that it was hidden from anyone looking in the area. He lifted the ladder back into the ceiling space and pushed it aside, towards the outside edge of the roof. He hoped that no-one would look towards the external side of the building. Once he had carried out a final check, he finally dropped into the bedroom space.

Greg, said under his breath, "Stage two completed, two more to go."

They then unzipped the bags to view the proceeds of their efforts. For three light-weight cons had never seen what a $1.4 million looked like, they were jubilant. They took beers out of the fridge to celebrate, and they tasted good. For a moment, their achievement seemed to give them a bond of friendship.

Chapter 38

Whilst all the euphoria was taking place, Greg realised that his problems had only just began, and a wave of anxiety flooded his thoughts as if he were back in Frackville and his immediate safety was in danger.

He knew that these two thugs, who he barely knew, had guns with them and he knew they would have been used before. Furthermore, there was $1.4 million sitting in the four bags. For most people, the sight of that much money would make them do irrational things, intentional or not. If he managed to avoid being shot and killed over the course of the next few hours, then there was a good possibility that he would be killed when he met-up with Mad Max tomorrow. It was not something that he was looking forward to.

He suddenly took a swig of beer and signalled to them that he was going to the toilet. Having closed the bathroom door, he opened the tap and ran the water. He removed the screwdriver from his pocket and bending down on one knee, he unscrewed the two screws that kept the side panel attached to the bath. He leant in and picked up the bag that had been placed there earlier in the afternoon. He took out the Berretta Model 70 handgun and slipped-on the suppressor attachment. Once he switched off the water, he flushed the toilet then headed back into the bedroom.

In the bedroom, both Franco and Roberto were lying on the bed, still with big grins on their faces, leaning on the backrest of the double bed. Greg casually walked up to them, lifted the gun and shot one and then the other, through the centre of their foreheads.

Franco and Roberto had no time to react and it was all over for them in an instant. Besides the homeless drunk that he had unintentionally killed, this was the first time he had killed anyone, let alone executed them in cold blood. It was easier than he thought, perhaps his time in Frackville hadn't been wasted after all.

He finished his beer while he recollected his thoughts. He then sourced a sharp Stanley knife out of the bag, and in one movement, sliced the front of the overalls that one of the men wore down the whole length. He repeated the same on the other side. He then semi-rolled the body over and pulled the sliced overalls from underneath, which came off the dead body easily. He did the same with the underpants before placing all the clothing into a refuse bag. He repeated the same procedure with the second body.

When both bodies were naked, he placed his fingers, one on the top eyelid, and the other at the bottom, then pushed his fingers into the back of the eye socket. The eyeball popped out, after which he used the sharp knife to cut any muscle strands attached, and then the cornea, at the back of the eyeball. He dropped the eyeball into the refuse bag and repeated the same procedure with the other three eyes.

Once finished, he took the heavy-duty bolt cutters out of the tool bag. Using the cutters, detached all the fingers from the hands of both bodies. Once again, he placed them in the refuse bag. As he would have to sleep with them for the rest of the morning, he decided to cover-up their naked bodies with a blanket.

He spent the next hour securing the ceiling hatch door, cleaning-up and making sure no trace of evidence was left behind. He also transferred all the money in the collapsible bags into the three solid, empty suitcases that had been on the luggage trolley. The last thing he did was write 'Bastard' on the mirror with lipstick, hoping that this would fool the crime investigators into thinking that the murders may have been a gay lover's revenge.

Looking at his watch, he realised that it was four o'clock, and he had two hours to get some rest. It was then time to execute stage four, the exit of the Rivonia.

Chapter 39

The alarm went off and Greg saw that it was 06.00. He got up, checked that his friends had not moved overnight and quickly washed his face in the bathroom. He then removed his own overalls, gloves, and skull cap, placing them in the common refuse bag, which he then sealed. He changed into his own clothing, including a casual jacket and hat to prevent his face being detected on CCTV. Having scanned both the bedroom and the bathroom for the last time, he then left the room and headed for the reception area to check-out.

Taking with him the transportable luggage trolley, which contained the $1.4 million in the suitcases and the refuse bags, he approached the reception area where the night porter was still on duty. However, as his room was already paid for, he didn't need to check-out or talk to the porter. He simply dropped off the two card keys and walked out through the club exit.

The car-jockey was not on duty yet, so Greg went unnoticed as he walked a short distance to the general car park to his white Ford SUV, where he loaded the suitcases and the refuse bags into the back of the trunk. Having dumped the luggage trolley, he then got in his car and drove out of the Rivonia. "Stage four now complete." he said under his breath.

At 07.30, using Franco's phone, he sent a text message to Mad Max. Then at 08.30, he phoned the Harrisburg police bureau and passed his message on to Irene.

Not wanting to be shot in the back of the head, Greg had no intention of meeting Max at the motel. So, he headed home, via the municipality refuse tip to drop off some unwanted refuse bags.

The next day his plans were to visit his mother and take her to Disney Land, in Orlando, a holiday that she had always promised him if she won the lottery. Then, he was going to buy her a small condo and make sure that she had enough money so she never had to work again. He was also planning to donate half of his recently gained riches to a homeless charity in Harrisburg. The redistirbution of his financial rewards for those more in need, would give him the most satisfaction.

Chapter 40

After his visit to Greg Johnson's business unit a few days ago and having discovered that he had disappeared into thin air, curiosity got the better of Dan. He decided that he needed a break, so he booked into the local country club for the night.

The next day, he arrived at the reception of the Rivonia where the receptionist confirmed his name and his room, which had been previously requested. Having informed the porter that he didn't need help, he pushed his luggage trolley to room 215.

Upon entering the bedroom, he was slightly hesitant, as unpleasant memories of his previous visits suddenly flooded back to him. He was relieved to find that he was the only occupant in the room.

After hanging up his clothes, he left the room and went for a walk around the club public areas, stopping at the bar where he had a relaxing drink. He spent some time observing the passing parade, then finished his drink and headed back to his room.

On the way back, he walked past room 212, which still appeared to be heavily locked, suggesting that the room was still being used as a secure safe room. He entered his bedroom, room 215, making sure that the door was locked behind him. Unzipping his suit cover, which contained a foldable ladder that he had purchased earlier from a local hardware store, he then removed and extended the ladder to full-length. He wondered if Greg had also done something like this as well.

He leant the ladder up against the wall alongside the ceiling access hatch, climbed up, removed the screwdriver from his pocket, and unscrewed the four screws. Once these screws were removed, the access hatch door fell-open on its hinges. He switched on his LED flashlight and put his head through into the ceiling space.

The first thing he noticed was that the space above the hatch was not obstructed like the others that he had previously seen. An average-sized adult could climb through into the ceiling area. So, he lifted himself up, and sitting on the edge of the frame of the hatch access door, he looked around the space with his flashlight.

He noted that all the other ceiling hatch doors had service pipes located directly above the hatch space, so that any access past the pipes was limited. However, for room 215, the service pipes appeared to have been altered in the shape of a U-bend, providing a free-space for someone to climb into the area.

Having a closer look, he noticed that the direction of the pipes had been altered recently, and it looked as though it had been intentional. "Had Greg Johnson done this? After all, he was a pipe and valve man." he thought with a smile on his face.

He then entered the space, balancing himself on the horizontal joists and crawled for a short distance towards the centre of the building. Once he was in the centre, he stood up and with the help of his flashlight, had a look around the space.

He made his way to room 212, the safe secure room, which was easy to identify as it was covered in white, fire-retardant boarding. He looked at the ventilation supply ducting to the room and saw that it came in sections, and the right-angled bend near the air discharge grille could be easily removed. There were in total, eight bolts and nuts and once removed, this section could be lifted and moved aside. Once this section had been removed, they would have had straightforward access to the ceiling grille. They wouldn't have had to navigate around a ninety-degree bend, as he had previously thought.

He thought to himself, "Having removed the ducting section, then the plastic ceiling grille, and using the ladder that he just climbed up with, they could then lower the ladder into the secure area. Having secured the ladder, they could climb down and open-up the money boxes, fill-up the collapsible bags, and then climb back up the ladder. Once back in the ceiling void, they would have replaced the grille and re-secured the ductwork, before heading back to the room. The sequence of scenarios all now made sense."

On his way back to room 212, something caught his eye, and he noticed that there were six long rectangular ply-wood boards. No other room appeared to have them, and they looked new. "Were these boards there to make sure that they did not fall through the ceiling boards, and to help them transport the money back from room 212?" he wondered.

He also noticed a protruding nail on one of the vertical joists, which had a piece of torn cloth attached and some blood on the fabric. "Was this the cut on the upper arm of the victim that was found in the autopsy?" he thought.

He had seen enough and once back at room 212, he climbed down the ladder, closing the ceiling hatch behind him. He noticed that there was nothing wrong with the hatch door latch and it didn't require screwing down in place, suggesting that Greg had done this deliberately. Once back in the room, he pulled up the chair and sat there looking at the double bed.

The next question was, why did he kill them? The only conclusion Dan could come up with was that he knew that his partners in crime were well-known killers, who were armed, and with $1.4 million sitting in the room, that there was no way he was going to survive the next few hours alive.

When they arrested Max, in his bedroom at the Gardens, he had a gun alongside him suggesting that Greg would have been eventually killed. Having weighed up his options, which were heavily stacked against him, he must have decided to kill them himself, setting Max up along the way. He would have known that while Max was in jail, he would not come after him to retrieve the money or avenge the death of his associates.

He left the room and went for a well-deserved beer at the bar. During his drink, he silently smiled and appreciatively nodded his head. He had finally cracked the Rivonia crimes and had figured out how Greg had done it, which was all a relief for him and no more restless nights.

Reflecting on the case; if, at the time, he had sent forensics up into the ceiling area for a sweep, they would have picked up the blood on the cloth attached to the nail which would have linked the two crime scenes. We could have also traced the purchase of the rectangular boards back to one of the local hardware stores in town. Additionally, he was sure that the boards would have contained the only fingerprints of the crime scene, those of Victor Stanley, alias Greg Johnson.

They had spent so much time and effort thinking that it was an 'inside-job' due to the lack of evidence. The removal of the eyeballs, and fingers, suggested that it was a professional 'hit-job' and it meant that they had no traceable evidence to work with. This also had us thinking that Franco had done the killings. He had to accept that two perfect crimes had taken place. You can't solve criminal cases if you have no hard evidence.

He could imagine Greg, sitting on the same barstool, observing the money box arriving to collect the takings for the evening, knowing all along he had a cunning plan to break into the Rivonia safe secure area.

The plan was brilliant, yet so simple, and Greg was the only person in the world who knew how to access the area. He was a genius.

The good news was that there were now two people in the world who knew how to access the Rivonia safe secure room, and if he was ever short of cash, he may consider a robbery sometime.

PART TWO

FIVE YEAR LATER

Chapter 41

Former Chief Detective Dan Liebenberg had been retired from the Harrisburg Major Crimes and Homicide Division for the past five years. He found retirement to be boring missing the social interaction of the workplace, good or bad. He hated being alone and longed for the office environment and the few beers after work.

Spending time with people who were not ex-policemen was always a challenge for him, as he never really had anything in common with them. It might have helped to have a female companion in his life, however, Dan had long given up the thought of sharing his life with someone else. The two divorces that he'd been through, along with years of poor financial management, meant that he still had personal debt even through his retirement. After he had paid off his monthly outgoings, the police pension barely covered his daily entertainment budget, which he mostly spent at the golf course clubhouse. Sharing his pension with another meant that he would've had to give up his only remaining indulgences.

On most days Dan followed the same routine, wake up, walk the dog, eat breakfast and then decide who he would call to suggest another game of golf. On other days, he would have a change in routine and go fishing. Although he enjoyed fishing, it was not the same when there was no one to talk to over a beer.

Dan had started to become depressed, and knew that he was drinking more than he should be. Playing golf with his friends was his only interaction that he had with others. As time went on, he became aware that he was drinking more than the odd one-or-two in the clubhouse before driving home. Furthermore, he recognised that drinking and then driving his car was a terrible idea, but he did it anyway. He figured that if he were ever caught, one of his old colleagues would let him off.

For many retirees, the Wednesday evening golf competition was always a good day out that stretched into the evening. That evening was the same as any other, and the socialising in the bar extended late into the night. When he arrived at his car in the car park, around 10.00 pm, Dan was obviously drunk, but didn't really appreciate his state. He managed to navigate the first ten miles successfully, without hitting anything, and only needed to make the last few miles before getting home. However, it was not to be.

The poorly lit road near Dan's home twisted and turned, making the journey all the more treacherous. Having gone around one of the corners, he saw a large deer standing there in front of his car. The deer, blinded by the car lights, stared at him in shock, frozen to the spot. To avoid the deer, Dan yanked on the steering wheel. However, his sudden attempt to avoid the deer led to him overcompensating, causing the car to swerve in the opposite direction. It catapulted into the air, rotating at least three times, before coming to an abrupt stop when it hit a tree. He hadn't even missed the deer, which gasped out its final breaths before dying.

Dan could not remember much, as he had passed out and finally woke up in a local hospital ICU the next morning. There, the doctor informed him that he had suffered multiple fractures of the legs and arms. Some would say he was lucky. Others would say that if he hadn't drunk so much, he could have avoided the crash. Dan was just grateful to be alive.

Luckily for him, there were no other third-parties involved in the accident. Besides his wounded ego, Dan had also written off his beloved Buick LeSabre. Still, the car was now over 20 years old, meaning that it was high time that he purchased a new car. Although, it would have to be second-hand. Dan's concern was that he had limited savings and trying to purchase a car would involve a bank loan. His crash meant that he was just about to extend his debt obligations, even further. His alcoholic self-indulgence on that night had proved costly.

Whilst he was on the mend, Dan's time was taken up with intensive physical therapy at the local hospital. For the next three months, it meant that there were few opportunities to go fishing, let alone golfing. He instead spent his time reading and procrastinating about all the chores that he'd abandoned.

Over time, possibly due to his newly acquired lifestyle, he discovered that he had Type-2 diabetes and now required a regular dose of insulin. Insulin in the USA being as infamously expensive as it was, Dan soon found that his retirement income barely covered the cost of his much-needed insulin. Medical aid schemes in the USA weren't fair on those who needed them most.

Dan realised that he needed to change his present routine as the outlook did not look promising. Any form of happiness or enjoyment was not on the agenda as they cost money that he simply didn't have. Dan's boredom and the need to change his lifestyle meant that he had no option but to look for employment. Furthermore, he needed to find work with a company that would pay his medical bills. Dan decided that he was too young to retire just yet and could get, at least, another five years' worth of work which would hopefully put him in a better financial position for when he re-entered retirement.

Out of the blue, an old colleague gave Dan a call and asked him whether he would be interested in a job in the commercial sector. The services of highly experienced ex-policemen were always in demand for companies looking to employ people in the security sector. As he had previously held the position of Head of Homicide in Harrisburg for most of his working life, Dan's future employment was guaranteed, if he wanted to go into the commercial sector, that is.

The main attraction of the offered position was that the salary package was almost twice his previous annual salary and with full medical insurance. It sounded too good to be true and would remove his boredom while relieving Dan's tricky financial position.

The only down-side was that the position was based in Dubai. Having not experienced much international travel before, the position was an attractive option for Dan, it was an opportunity to see another country and to experience the local culture.

After some thought, Dan decided that he had no alternative but to attend the job interview.

Chapter 42

The interview took place in New York in an upmarket commercial building. The company was an American corporation called ACE FM and they specialised in facilities management. They were a global company with offices in most countries and they looked after the facilities management of over 10,000 commercial office buildings. They employed a workforce of over 20,000 staff including operations managers, building engineers, security, and cleaners.

The client, the Emirates Real Estate, was a commercial financial fund, an investment arm for the royal family. They owned fifty buildings in Dubai, including modern commercial offices, hotels, and shopping centres. Their total asset value was in the region of $2 trillion and they were considered one of the major players in the commercial real estate market throughout the Middle East. If any new real estate developments were taking place, they would be at the table. At any one time, they were involved in two or three new building projects that would reshape the Dubai landscape for years to come. ACE FM had won a three year facilities management contract for all their sites in Dubai, ensuring that their buildings were well operated and maintained.

The Facilities Management Company would, on behalf of the owner, oversee the safe operation of all mechanical and electrical services in their buildings, including the ventilation and A/C systems. Its services would also include providing security for the building, and the front-of-house operations, such as the reception area. Their duties would include dealing with the ongoing operations and maintenance of all facilities within the building, as well as daily complaints from the tenants. In short, if you wanted a light bulb changed, you contacted the local ACE help desk, who would then delegate the local building engineer to fix the issue.

They wanted Dan to head up the security for the Middle East region. The issue highlighted to him was that theft and corruption were rife in the region. A simple job like changing a light bulb could cost 500 to 600% more than it should.

There were two types of 'kick-backs'. One was internal, where a secret exchange took place between the senior person signing off the contract and the contractor providing the service. The third-party contractor nominated for the job would 'load' the price, and then it would be signed off. Once complete, either the building manager or the local engineer would receive his 'wedge', a commission for his participation.

The other involved an external third-party, the 'deal maker', a middle-man. There was a large group of individuals who got a 'wedge' by providing the connection. Most of these deal makers had never worked a full day in their lives and brought no expertise to the table, yet they were highly respected throughout the business community. Dubai was full of them.

For a company like ACE, it did not matter what governance policies or anti-corruption training were in place for your staff. It was a generally accepted practice for your employees to be always looking to financially benefit themselves, even at the expense of the owners. Any external contractors providing a service knew that they would have to pay a 'wedge' to get the contract. In Dubai, these transactions were basically a local custom, they were needed to get anything done. It was estimated that at least 90% of all facilities service contracts were 'loaded'.

The result was that both the owner and the facilities management companies were being ripped-off, mostly by their own staff. Typically, over the period of the contract, this would result in a surplus of millions of dollars that the client, the building owner, had to pay. This led to mistrust between the owner and the facilities management company and often, the eventual loss of the contract at the end of its term.

Another issue was that the facility management service contracts only lasted for three years. The short-term culture fostered no loyalty or interest in creating a long-term working partnership. It didn't help that the clients wanted the work to be done more cheaply than the previous contract. So, to make a profit, everyone cut corners, trying to offer the same service but at a lower contract cost. This created a terrible, non-productive working environment and was a major issue in the facility management industry.

Employing local staff in middle management positions was a recipe for disaster, as in most cases, the issue was that they were the cause of much of the theft and corruption. The only recognised way of sorting out the corruption was to employ someone who had a moral compass and recognised social and ethical standards. You had to import key staff in management positions, such as Dan, the ex-Head of Homicide, from Harrisburg in America.

His job was to clean up the widespread corruption within the region and to install governance and reporting systems that made sure that these practices did not take place within the buildings that the company managed. As the 'wedge' culture was well established, some would say that he was taking on an impossible mission.

Chapter 43

Dan had a month to sort out his personal issues, which included re-homing his faithful dog, organising someone to keep an eye on his house and water his plants, and saying good-byes to all his friends. He also took the opportunity to clear out all the old possessions that he had been meaning to get rid of for years now. On the day, he got a friend to take him to the airport.

Once on board, Dan realised that this was the first long-haul international flight that he had ever been on. During the flight, whilst taking advantage of the free drinks in the Business class section, he realised that he had lived a sad, uneventful life. He had been stuck in Harrisburg all his life, having never had the opportunity to travel, being constantly broke. His annual leave was mostly taken up with fishing trips and other dull events. Most of his holidays had never been planned, left to the last moment, usually on a Friday afternoon in the bar, the day before he went on holiday. Every opportunity to broaden his horizon, to make his life more meaningful, had been wasted.

No wonder the local ladies did not consider him a catch, he thought, swigging down another whiskey, trying to get rid of his self-pity.

Arriving in Dubai, the outside temperature approaching 50°C, left Dan shell-shocked, as he had never before experienced anything like this. The outside heat was intense and unrelenting. The time of day didn't matter, you needed to find somewhere with air-conditioning for any relief to the senses.

Although Harrisburg had some large commercial buildings, they were nothing like Dubai. Dan marvelled at the sheer size of the buildings and wondered how they had even come to exist in the middle of a desert. The opulence and outrageous architectural designs belonged to another time, as if they had left the rest of the world behind. When it came to modern, brash building structures, nothing compared to Dubai.

He had always thought that the local traffic in Harrisburg was bad, but soon discovered that Dubai was even more hectic, it was off the scales. The locals drove their cars like adrenaline junkies, guided by their inflated egos and lack of common sense. You constantly needed to be on high alert and even a short drive left you exhausted, taking hours longer than it should.

The migrant population consisted of around 80% of the total working population of Dubai. The city could not have been built, let alone function, if not for the low-salaried, hardworking immigrants. This melting pot of different nationalities, with diverse moral and social standards, resulted in an insular society where real friends were hard to find. You were in Dubai to work, leaving little time for socialising. This was good news for Dan's liver, at least, as his alcohol consumption was now non-existent.

Once he had settled into his new role, Dan soon learnt the local customs and behaviours. He found that dealing with the locals was a challenge. Dan developed a simple attitude to meeting someone in Dubai. You always thought the worst of them and that they were almost guaranteed to let you down. You did not give them the benefit of the doubt, and no-one could be trusted. They were all potential back-stabbers looking for an opportunity to gain a financial or psychological advantage over you. Over time, you learnt to identify who could be trusted. Still, this trust could be dissolved in a minute, depending on the size of the bribe.

Dan soon learnt that the position that he had taken on was wide and diverse and certainly a challenge. He had to work long hours, as this was the only way of keeping on top of the demanding job. However, he was not the only one working so hard, everyone in Dubai needed to go the extra mile to guarantee their employment.

Chapter 44

Dan had been in Dubai for over a year and had settled into a routine. Most days would consist of getting up at 05.00, so that he could be on the road by 05.30, to hopefully avoid the traffic. However, once on the road, he would soon notice that half of Dubai had the same idea as him. The trip to the office would usually take ninety minutes. The same trip, if carried out an hour later, would take him 120 minutes, if he were lucky.

He often thought about his working career in Harrisburg, where the pace was typically slower, and he had a more relaxed lifestyle. At the end of the day, he still had time to socialise with friends and, occasionally, enjoy a quick game of golf. Spending around three hours daily on the road meant that there was no time for anything like exercise or other beneficial pastimes. People were expected to work twelve hours every day, six days a week. It was like an unstoppable treadmill, and once on, your time and existence belonged to others.

Dan's office was located near the main business centre, a modern building, with external walls consisting of full-length glass, the height of the building. The building, along with the surrounding identical buildings, were large, air-conditioned glass houses containing thousands of hard-working employees. His office was situated on the 10th floor with good views of downtown Dubai, the sea in the distance.

His security team consisted of five staff with varying security experience and a mix of nationalities. His able assistant was called David Brown, a retired policeman from West Yorkshire, in the north of England. He was tall and lanky, with an easy smile.

As they were the only two native English speaking members of staff, they soon became good friends. However, Dan would confess that there were times when he couldn't understand David's Yorkshire accent.

The local staff called them Mr Dan and Mr David. This was an informal, local custom that suggested that they could not be bothered to find out their surnames. Dan and David both found this amusing, so they called each other the same thing.

Their typical day consisted of meetings, reviewing of security measures, investigating potential thefts, and interrogating staff members. Trying to spot and track any corruption taking place was a challenge, as all financial transactions were done in cash, most of it never deposited into a bank, making it untraceable. So, there was no clear evidence that could be used to prosecute the individual, who in most cases was an employee.

However, dismissing employees wasn't an issue, thanks to the lax employment regulations. If one suspected that theft had taken place, you simply terminated the suspect's employment. These lax labour laws designed to favour the employer created an environment of fear for most workers who knew that they were dispensable and could be discarded in an instant.

Chapter 45

For the majority of people working in Dubai, Friday was the only recognised day off during the week. Most of the commercial buildings would be empty of tenants. During this time, the ACE office help-desks were manned by limited staff who sorted out any building related issues that could arise on the day.

The text came through on Friday morning, around 12.00. Mohammed, the assistant manning the help-desk read it. It said,

"We are informing you that five of the Emirates Real Estate buildings are now under our control. If the owners do not pay a ransom of $100 million by 22.00, this evening, major fires shall take place in these buildings over the course of the next 24 hours."

Having seen the message, Mohammed's first reaction was to forward the text onto Dan, his Head of Security, who was at home, reading a book at the time. Dan casually picked up his phone, hoping that the text message was from David, perhaps suggesting that they meet up for a beer.

Instead, he had to read the message twice, not believing the message the first time.

"What the hell is this all about?" he thought. He gave Mohammad a quick call to inform him that he was on his way and that he was to contact Mr. David.

Within minutes, Dan was in his company-provided Toyota car and was headed towards the office. The traffic was not as bad as usual, and he was there only an hour later. On the way, he figured that each building had to be worth over $500 million in asset worth. That meant that five buildings had a potential value of over $2.5 billion. So the $100 million ransom was not much to ask, he thought, a smile on his face. Dan was trying to see a positive from a deadly serious situation.

He hadn't ever heard of a commercial building being held to ransom. You don't get ransom demands for buildings in Harrisburg, even if they were worth anything. Dan knew that this was going to be another long, challenging day.

When he got to his office, Dan met David in the meeting room, which had now become their centre of operations for the investigation, their emergency response room. Dan and David took another look at the text message, and Dan asked, "What do you think? Do you think it's a real threat? Have we had anything like this before?"

David shook his head, "I have never heard of a building being taken over like this. We don't have any high-rise buildings where I come from, never mind someone asking for a ransom. How the hell can someone, or even a group, take over a building?"

Ausaf, the lead engineering supervisor, arrived at the office. David pointed towards the text message and said, "What do you think about this then, Ausaf?"

"Yes, it might be possible that someone, or a group, could take over a building and demand a ransom," he said. It sounded like an obvious answer, as though he wanted to hedge his bets. Although Ausaf was the lead engineer supervisor, this did not necessarily mean that he had a full grasp of the extent of the potential issue. The person responsible didn't always have the necessary skills or competency for the job. Another misconception that Dan had learnt in Dubai.

Dan challenged him, "so, how would you do that then?"

Ausaf said nothing to confirm his statement.

On the wall-mounted board in the meeting room, Dan picked up a marker-pen, and wrote down the following three headings;

'who is doing it', 'how could they do it' and 'emergency response".

Under the 'who is doing it' he wrote down the obvious suspects, such as terrorist extremist groups. In brackets, Dan put "Al-Qaeda". He also included anti-capitalist groups, past business competitors, and cyber-hackers.

They could not rule out the possibility that a terrorist group was responsible. They were, after all, located in the epicentre of extremism, the Middle East. However, most terrorist groups were keen to make their involvement known, as this was their primary method of brainwashing the next generation of wannabe fanatics. The ransom demand did not come with a name, not that this meant that they wouldn't let the world know once the ransom was paid in full.

Could a terrorist group have placed time-controlled bombs in the various buildings? They would have had to get access to buildings which were highly secure and manned by local security staff. Strapping a bomb onto a poor helpless woman and forcing her to walk into a crowded market before detonating the device required less planning. Any psychopath could do that. However, they had managed to fly two jumbo jets into the Empire State buildings, suggesting that they could carry out more complex tasks if so motivated.

It might have been an anti-capitalism, or an environmentalist group, such as Extinction Rebellion, a protest group that had recently caused major disruption in London. However, typically the members of those groups tended to barricade or attach themselves to buildings. They generally made a lot of noise to get the maximum exposure in an attempt to make people more aware of climate change. Up to now, they had never asked for ransom demands. Still, perhaps their modus operandi had changed to generate more publicity.

Or these were everyday professional 'hackers', who had nothing better to do all day. It was well known that hackers had been responsible for several government attacks over the years. The buildings could have been the victims of a cyber-attack, perhaps perpetrated by Chinese or Russian hackers.

David said to Dan, "is this the latest trend, taking over buildings that have weak software access protocols, then demanding a ransom?"

It was also possible that the takeover of the buildings was related to an old fall-out over a business deal that had gone wrong. Perhaps it was revenge for a misdeed, which was a common practice in the Middle East. The locals tended to throw the 'dummy out of the cot' if it was perceived that they, or their family, had been dishonoured for whatever reason. The only person who could tell them this was the owners, but they wouldn't necessarily volunteer such information.

David suggested, "What about disgruntled past employees?"

"Good point," said Dan, and added it to the board.

As most employees working in Dubai were so aggrieved with their working conditions and how they were treated, they could easily be paid off, if the money were right. Maybe they handed over the usernames and passwords, along with some basic instructions on how to disable the software systems. An amateur IT operator could have then done the deed, working on behalf of a terrorist group. They did not necessarily need to have an in-depth understanding of the building systems.

They both agreed that the likelihood of an ex-employee being responsible could be very high, due to the high turnover of staff. However, most of the employees were semi-skilled, without the needed technical knowledge to carry out something like this. It could also be the local management within the buildings.

They had access to the building software systems and knew the passcodes.

One further thought was that this could be politically motivated. The owners were closely connected to the rulers of the kingdom. Although the excesses of Dubai were well known, and often overlooked by their neighbouring countries, it did not mean they agreed with them. If this was the case, then should this investigation be handed over to the government crime fighting agencies?

Under the 'how could they do it' heading, Dan wrote down time-controlled bombs located in an area in the building. Although all entrances to the buildings had metal detection equipment, could the bomb have been planted by a mechanical contractor who had disguised the device as equipment that he needed on site? Or maybe the local security manager on duty at the time had been paid off with a bribe to look the other way.

They also considered a possible direct missile strike, or similar military intervention. Still, the message did say that the perpetrators had taken over the building itself. Someone with an over-the-shoulder missile launcher, standing on the other side of the street with a cigarette in the side of his mouth, did not necessarily have to take over the building.

He also added the potential of a cyber-attack of the building mechanical and electrical operational software. Could this threat have come from one of their employees, or external contractors? Typcally, cyber-attacks switch off or cripple software systems. They don't start fires, especially not in empty buildings. The message specifically mentioned that a fire was to take place. They would need to identify the companies that installed and maintained this equipment.

They knew that this was all speculation, and hoped that once the first attack took place, they would have a better understanding of who had done this and how.

Under the 'emergency response' heading, Dan listed: lock-down all buildings, instruct on-duty security managers to have a walk-around to look for suspicious packages, such as something that looked like a bomb.

As it was a Friday, most of the buildings would have been in semi-lock down anyway. All external doors would have been closed, making them inaccessible to the general public. A local security guard would be monitoring the CCTV cameras, which covered most of the entrances to the building. They should have been able to identify a suspicious person and then notify the local police.

The issue was that there were fifty buildings in Dubai that were potential targets, and they had no idea which ones were under threat. Referring to the corporate asset list they had, there were several hotels that were occupied by guests. Would they target these sites for maximum exposure? There were also several out-of-town retail centres under consideration. However, their financial value was minimal compared to an office building in the middle of Dubai.

The threat came with no location, no motive or justification, nor anyone claiming responsibility. Furthermore, why select a day of the week when there were hardly any tenants in the offices?

They agreed that only once they knew how the attack took place, could they have a better idea of what emergency response would be appropriate.

Dan shook his head in amazement and said, "where do we even start with this investigation?"

Hopefully, in the next few hours, they would know more about the threat, and whether it was real or not.

Chapter 46

Rahul Patel, an Indian migrant, was the security manager for Arabian Gulf Plaza on the day. He had just left the air-conditioned reception room to have a well-deserved cigarette break. As he stepped out, he felt the immediate effect and the discomfort of the intense Dubai heat, which was now 50°C.

He had always questioned why anyone would want to indulge in their cigarette addiction, when they had to face the unbearable heat for just a few seconds of satisfaction. You did not need the latest non-smoking fads, such as nicotine patches, to stop the unhealthy habit. The extreme heat should have been enough for anyone to stop. But Rahul had been saying this for close to two years now, and it still didn't stop him from indulging himself.

He was relieved to get back into the building and re-seat himself at the reception desk. He enjoyed working on a Friday as it was a holiday, so there would be no-one in the building. He had the whole building to himself, with limited tasks, and no complaints from the tenants.

A short time later, Rahul noticed that the temperature in the reception area was starting to get warmer and more uncomfortable. He turned to his PC screen and opened up the building management software controls. He sourced the reception page, then clicked on the icon which showed him the operating data for the area. The area temperature readout showed that it was 26°C. In most buildings, the ambient temperature should be around 20°C.

His immediate reaction was to alter the temperature manually, on the screen. With a few clicks of his mouse, Rahul attempted to lower the temperature set-point of the area. He'd done this procedure countless times before. However, as soon as he appeared to have carried out the simple alteration, the set-point would default back to the present temperature. The software appeared to be malfunctioning, as the temperature digital indicator continued to display the rising heat.

This suggested that the main air-conditioning (A/C) plant was not working. Rahul headed for the lift, and once inside, pushed the button for the top floor, the roof area. A few minutes later, he left the lift. He opened the roof access door and went to the main A/C mechanical plant. Standing in front of the units, Rahul noticed that they were not operating as they should. It appeared that they had all been switched off. He tried repeatedly pushing a green button on the console, hoping to start the system. His attempts were in vain, they were still idle.

In an instant, Rahul knew that they had a serious issue. He did not need to be a qualified building engineer to recognise that a building with no air-conditioning was critical, especially when there was an outside temperature of 50°C. He spun around and headed back into the building and took the lift back to the reception area.

When he re-entered the reception area, Rahul was met with an even higher temperature than before. "Oh my god." He said to himself. He looked at the PC screen again, noticing that the temperature was now approaching 35°C. He began to sweat profusely and knew that he needed to get out of the building into the fresh air and make some urgent calls.

Once outside, he contacted the Westminster Controls help-desk, the maintenance contractor for the building software controls. No one answered his plea for help, so he left a message. A few minutes later, Rahul tried again. Once again, he had no luck getting through to another human being on the other side of the phone.

He then phoned the ACE help-desk, which went straight to the answering service. He left another urgent message.

Rahul's next action was to phone his Facilities Manager, his immediate superior. The telephone rang and rang, but still no answer. Once again, he left an urgent message on the answer machine.

Rahul's stress levels rose at an alarming rate. He knew that he was responsible for the building on the day, but there was nothing that he could do to remedy the issue.

To get some relief from the harsh midday sun, Rahul walked over to the other side of the road and found a bench sat beneath a tree. Once seated under the shade of the tree, he took out a stress-relieving cigarette and had a deep breath of nicotine which filled his lungs and immediately calmed his nerves. He looked at the building and reflected on his current circumstances.

Rahul said to himself. "It is Friday, and everyone is on holiday. No one will answer my phone calls. What am I supposed to do?"

Then, he smiled, as some do when they're in a helpless position and there's nothing that they can do to solve their problem. Once more, Rahul picked up his phone and tried contacting the help-desks. Someone at the ACE help-desk finally got back to him and he was told that the request had been escalated to another level, and that the maintenance contractors for the building were being notified.

There was nothing that he could do but wait. He decided to fill his time by phoning family and friends to try and explain his situation, hoping that they could provide a solution to the issue he had. Their advice was all in vain.

Chapter 47

Dan and his team, back in the emergency response room, soon came up with a plan. They concentrated on the commercial office buildings in the middle of Dubai, believing that their asset financial worth would be the main motivation for the perpetrators.

Through the next thirty minutes, emails were sent out to all building security managers and frantic calls were exchanged. All security managers presently on duty at each site, were to evacuate all occupants and lock down their building. They were to report any entries by third parties into the building in the past 24 hours. Also, they were to carry out a building walk around to spot anything that was out of the ordinary, such as suspicious packages that may have been left on site, either intentionally or not.

Dan and David knew that the external public entrances to these buildings were highly restricted and secure. Also, most of these buildings had metal detectors, so anyone entering a building with a bomb or similar device should have been picked up by the local security. However, some of the building's back entrances, for their staff and external contractors, may not be as well-manned or have the same level of security.

Within an hour, most had reported back that they had not noted any unauthorised entrance and that there did not appear any suspicious packages. Dan did appreciate that asking the local staff to find a potential bomb likely wouldn't have the desired results. These packages came in different sizes and shapes, and without appropriate training, the chances of your recently appointed amateur bomb-detector identifying the object were low. Furthermore, there were thousands of places where a bomb could be hidden in a building.

There was no response from the Arabian Gulf Plaza building as the security manager was not in the building at the time.

Dan said to David, "if it does not appear to be any suspect packages in the buildings, could this be a cyber-attack?"

David responded, "I agree. However, we have over fifty buildings. That means that there are a lot of places to hide a bomb."

Dan though about this for a while and replied, "For now, let's consider the fact that this could be a cyber-attack."

Dan wanted to arrange a conference call with the local building software providers for the buildings to get some indication of whether someone, or a group, could hack into the IT systems, and more importantly, what possible damage they could cause.

Dan turned to Ausaf and asked, "Who looks after the building management systems on our sites?"

Ausaf responded, "Well, there are a number of companies that we use," which was not what Dan wanted to hear.

Ausaf explained, "This isn't going to be easy, there are a range of contractors that we have used over the years. Each building has a different software system and, in most cases, the company who installed the system is long-gone, out of the picture."

He added, "We do have one or two companies where we have established relationships, but most they come and go, depending on who is in favour with senior management at the time."

Dan took one look at David, and both raised their eyebrows to confirm that this was not going to be straightforward, just like getting anything else done in Dubai.

"Furthermore," said Ausaf, "there is another problem. It's Friday, and most companies are having their day off."

Dan thought, as we all work like dogs for most of the week, it's going to be a challenge to get hold of someone to discuss the issue. David instructed Ausaf to provide a list of current contractors and to try and contact them.

The main issue that Dan had was what to do next. Should they contact the owners, or inform the police, and turn it into a full investigation? However, as nothing had taken place yet, they decided to delay these calls.

Dan knew that if he were to contact the owners, the immediate reaction would be to blame the security management of ACE FM. There was a blame culture in Dubai, everything was always someone else's fault. This resulted in no one taking responsibility. This could lead to dire consequences as pre-emptive or early solutions to problems were rarely attempted.

At this point, it wasn't clear what this group were planning to do or what their motive was. So, all they could do was wait and see what happened next. Dan would then contact the owners, and the police, when it happened.

Chapter 48

Around 14.00, as Rahul was having his fifth cigarette, he heard a thud and saw splinters of glass tumbling down from a high level before finally landing on the concrete at the building entrance. He looked up towards the fifteenth floor of the building. It was now obvious that the building was ablaze. It was time to get back on the telephone and contact the help-lines, as well as call the local fire department emergency response line.

While Rahul was frantically trying to get hold of the ACE help-desk, Dan received another text message from Mohammad. It read:

"The Arabian Gulf Plaza building is now on fire."

Dan and David looked at each other with one mind, the threat had now become real.

They walked over to the external office window to view the Arabian Gulf Plaza building, which was around five miles. Dan picked up a pair of binoculars and took a closer view. In the distance, he could see that the fifteenth floor of the Arabian Gulf Plaza building was in flames.

The Arabian Gulf Plaza was a high-rise commercial building situated in the middle of the business district of Dubai. It was over thirty-five years old and was, at the time, considered to be the crown in the Emirates Real Estate portfolio of buildings. It was still a well-recognised building even as bigger and more lavish commercial buildings had been built in Dubai. However, the Arabian Gulf Plaza was starting to show its age and had lost its reputation along the way.

"Oh my god, it's happening," said Dan, passing the binoculars over to David.

The building was worth an estimated $500 million, making this now a major crime scene. The local fire department was notified, and they were there in minutes. But the fire was on the fifteenth floor, making it nigh impossible to fight. The owners and key senior management in ACE were notified, their afternoon of relaxation with their families was soon to come to an end.

Dan looked at the notice board again. His main question was "How the hell did they start a fire on the fifteenth floor?"

Rahul had finally contacted the right person, someone who would take his urgent requests for help seriously. It had taken him close to two hours. Dan put Rahul onto the speaker phone in the meeting room.

Dan asked the first question, "Do we know how the fire started? Was there an explosion suggesting a bomb?"

Rahul responded. "No, I heard nothing, as I wasn't in the building when the fire took place."

This puzzled Dan and he asked, "Why not? That's your job. You are supposed to stay in the building at all times."

He replied, "Around two hours before the fire, the building started to get very, very hot. The internal temperature got so high that I had to leave the building."

"How hot?" asked David.

"The last time I looked it was 35°C, but then I had to get out. It was rising all the time."

"Why didn't you alter the temperature on the building management control system software?" asked Ausaf.

"I tried, I really did try to lower the temperature on the controls, but it just kept rising. It was like I had no control. Every time I tried to manually lower the temperature; it would default back to the higher value."

He added, "I went onto the roof to check the A/C plant, but the units were not working and I could not start them."

Rahul knew what was coming next.

Ausaf now shouted at Rahul, "Did you contact the A/C contractor helpdesk?"

By this time, Rahul was even more distressed than before and close to tears as he tried to explain away his perceived incompetence. "Yes, I did. But no one would take my call. I contacted everyone, the BMS man and the A/C Company."

"I left five messages, five messages," repeating himself, hoping to dissolve his responsibility.

"Did you contact anyone at the ACE out-of-hours help desk?"

"Yes, of course I did. I left messages on the answerphone and I was told that they would do something about it," he said.

"Did you tell them how important it was?" said Ausaf, raising his voice once again.

"Yes, I did. No one would listen to me," replied Rahul.

"You are the security manager on duty. You are responsible for what happens in the building. You should have made sure that it was reported," Ausaf said, pinning the blame on Rahul.

Ausaf had decided that Rahul, a poorly educated foreigner from India, employed as their building security manager, was entirely to blame for a burning $500 million building. Besides losing his job, he would be forever known as that security manager who had been responsible for the destruction of the Arabian Gulf Plaza, even though he hadn't started the fire.

David intervened, trying to bring the conversation back to something more meaningful, "Rahul, just to confirm, did you hear any explosions?"

Rahul responded, "No."

"Did you see anyone enter the building during the morning who may have looked suspicious, say, carrying a bag?"

"No", he replied, "other than a delivery person who dropped off a package for one of the tenants, I didn't see anyone else." He added, "He didn't enter the building and I signed for the package at the front."

"What was the package, how big was it?" asked David.

Rahul replied, "It was a small, soft, envelope sized package. It did not start the fire."

Dan asked, "So, Rahul just to confirm, when you tried to change the temperature set point, it would not respond?"

"Yes, there was nothing that I could do. Someone had switched off the air-conditioning and there was nothing I could do." He replied in vain.

Dan turned to his team, "Gents, it sounds like the building management control software has been overridden, possibly via a cyber-attack by a third-party."

Dan turned to Ausaf and asked, "If the internal temperature increases too greatly, and the building overheats, could it eventually catch fire?"

Ausaf replied, "It depends on how high the temperature gets, so it could possibly catch fire." It was an obvious answer and simple logic suggested that this could happen.

David looked at Dan and, pointing towards the Arabian Gulf Plaza building, said, "Well, we now have proof that increasing the building internal temperature causes fires."

Dan picked up the binoculars again and looked towards the building. It appeared that floors 15, 16 and 17 were now ablaze. The fire was spreading fast to the upper floors.

All commercial buildings had, by law, a quick response fire detection and extinguishing system on each floor. These systems were tested weekly. There was no reason why the systems should not have been working. So why was the fire not being extinguished?

Ausaf turned to Dan, "The fire is spreading fast. I think the fire detection and prevention software has been overridden as well."

"Oh my god," was all that David could manage to say, looking at Dan in astonishment.

Dan turned to the notice board and looked at the three headings; under 'who was doing it', they still did not know who was responsible. Under 'how they were doing it', they now had some idea, but needed urgent help from a software contractor to get a better understanding on how they could stop it.

Under the 'emergency response' heading, they now knew that locking down all the buildings would be pointless. It appeared that whoever was controlling these fires did not necessarily have to be at the scene. It was not a traditional fire, where the 'fire-starter' had a can of petrol and a match. It appeared that the buildings were being controlled by an external force, dictating what happens next. If someone had hacked into the building operating systems and then switched off the fire detection systems, there was nothing that the local security manager or the fire department could do to prevent the fire.

Dan's next move was to contact all security managers and get them to tell him when the building was heating up. This would give them time to notify the fire department and more importantly, to evacuate the building. However, when the building temperature reached 30°C, most people would automatically feel the discomfort and leave the building anyway.

As most of the Dubai fire department were fighting the Arabian Gulf Plaza building fire, giving them prior warning for a fire in another part of town would not be that beneficial. Even if they got to the building before the fire started, they might not be able to do anything to prevent it, especially if the fire detection systems had been switched off.

Although they had some idea what was taking place, a cyber-attack of the building management software, they needed to figure out how to prevent further attacks. Could they intervene and overcome the present scenario, to prevent further attacks? Only the software controls manufacturer, or the present maintenance contractor, could tell them this. They hoped that there was some way to override the software access that was presently controlled by the hacker, or hackers. Such a sophisticated operation suggested that more than one person was likely involved and potentially suggested a terrorist organisation with a network of dedicated loyalists on the ground.

It was obvious to both Dan and David that the present scenario was not favourable for them. There was no physical evidence available to help their investigation. There would be no forensic evidence such as fingerprints or DNA left at the scene. It appeared that they had a crime scene that was being carried out by invincible villains, who could be anywhere.

The next point that Dan wrote on the notice board was to contact the building management software contractors and try and understand what is going on. Unfortunately, these companies were on holiday and contacting them would be a challenge.

He then added another, one that he was dreading. Dan would have to contact the owners.

Chapter 49

Contacting the owner was not as easy as it sounded. First of all, they spoke limited English. In fact, Dan had never met them before. So they had to rely on the spokesman Josef, a senior manager for the group, to make contact. But even this wasn't straightforward, as the owners did not want to hear bad news. They employed people to do the work and delegated away all responsibility.

The owner was finally contacted. Josef, in an attempt to appease them and keep them calm, told them that everything was under control. That Mr Dan and Mr David were dealing with the situation and the fire department was at the scene extinguishing the fire.

This conversation was all conducted in a language that neither Dan nor David were familiar with. When Josef had finished speaking to the owner, Dan asked him to relay the content of the telephone call back to him.

After hearing his reply, Dan came to a quick conclusion. It was obvious that the true extent of the damage had been hidden. Furthermore, Josef, had conveniently not informed the owners of the ransom demand that had come with the original message. It had also sounded like that Dan was now solely responsible for the fire.

"Only in Dubai," Dan thought to himself. The present situation he found himself in hinted that he could be on a plane home to Harrisburg within a few days. The thought was an attractive one. As much as he wanted to be loyal and a dedicated member of staff, Dan knew that this meant nothing.

He turned to David, smiled and said, "I reckon we could be back home next week playing golf." David smiled back and said, "yes, you could be right'."

David then instructed Josef to re-contact the owners and inform them of the ransom demand, and that other buildings could be next. He stressed to Josef that they had no idea which building would be next, so the owner had no option but to consider paying the ransom.

Josef, reluctantly, phoned the owners again to inform them of the misinformation that he'd spread earlier. This resulted in a screaming match between the owner and Josef.

Josef came off the phone and was obviously not in a happy mood. The owners had questioned why the police had not been involved. This was a good point, however, as Dan had no way of knowing whether the ransom threat had been real, and the fire had only started fifteen minutes ago, that would be their next move.

Josef informed them that the owners, who had friends in higher places in the government, would be organising this. The special investigation squad was on their way.

Dan dreaded the thought of the local police getting involved with the investigation, as they could make things worse. When they arrived, he would have to hand over the investigation and he could foresee a catalogue of overreactions and miss-management taking place. Then again, this wasn't the worst fate, as he was about to be relieved of his responsibility. He had only been in Dubai for a year, but he was now thinking like the locals. At all times, look for an opportunity to disassociate yourself from any responsibility.

Chapter 50

A member of the ACE human resources arrived in the office and within minutes, they had a list of all present and ex-employees that had worked for ACE in the past three years. In total, they presently employed three hundred members of staff who looked after the fifty buildings in the portfolio. They were made up of senior management roles which headed up the key departments such as engineering, security, IT, human resources, and general administration.

The next level below was the Operation Managers who looked after around ten buildings each, and they oversaw the staff management, administration and acted as the liaison between the owner's representatives and the local staff. Each building had its own Facilities manager, who supervised the daily operation of the building, and dealing with tenant complaints. Typically, these managers had a management degree, or equivalent, or had worked their way up from being an engineer.

At the bottom of the food chain was the Building Engineers and every site had one. All things that were technically related was their responsibility. They made sure the building's mechanical and electrical systems operated as intended. Their duties were wide and diverse and would include all air-conditioning and heating plants, the ventilation systems, and the lifts. They were knowledgeable when it came to the building software control systems, so that various operating systems could be adjusted to improve the tenant comfort levels. When there were any technical issues, they were the ones who fixed them.

Most would say that they were the critical component in the chain of responsibility, yet, as they had achieved their education through apprenticeships and local colleges rather than being not university educated, they were not treated with the respect they deserved. This was due to the locals thinking that a university education meant not having to get their hands dirty. These engineering positions were filled with low-cost foreigners, mainly Filipinos and Indians.

Most were not real building engineers, as they were ex-electricians or plumbers who had decided to move from the domestic sector into the commercial one. It was an opportunity to improve their career prospects and it meant more pay than before. They were generally treated poorly and with the constant changing of contracts, there was little job loyalty. The result was that there were many disgruntled employees leading to a high turnover of staff.

Any specialist work that needed carrying out would be done by a local, external contractor, either the original manufacturer of the equipment or a local representative who would do the installation and maintenance. An example of this was the building management software (BMS) controls. The local Building Engineers understood how to alter the temperature and time settings, but not how to programme them. However, to get access to the software, they would have the username and passwords. One of these engineers might have been bribed to hand over these access codes to a third-party.

Dan and David looked at the responsibility structure and came to the conclusion that whoever the hacker was would have to understand the BMS software system. Looking down the management chain, they identified that a Building Engineer with some background knowledge of computer programming could potentially enter the system and change the passwords, so that no access could be gained by a third-party.

The advantage that the local Building Engineers had, when compared to the specialist software contractors, was that they knew about every other system in the building such as the fire detection and ventilation systems. The specialist contractors typically only concentrated on their area of expertise and did not necessarily know about how other building systems operated.

Between Dan and David, they decided that the person would have to be a specialist in BMS software systems and also know how the various mechanical and electrical systems worked and how they were integrated into the overall operation of the building. Furthermore, they would also have to have the courage to escalate the severity of their crime to the destruction of the building, and then demand a ransom.

Altering a software system to cause overheating in the building so that tenants had to leave the building, was one thing. Causing the total destruction of the building took it up a notch and they were potentially dealing with someone with psychopathic tendencies. Someone with a lack of feeling or empathy for their actions. This strongly suggested that the person may have belonged to a terrorist group or had similar goals.

Dan and David had now built up a physiological profile of the potential suspects. They decided to concentrate on the past and present Building Engineers and the external contractors who worked for the BMS software companies. Looking down the list of employees, present and past, they saw close to one hundred Building Engineers that would need to be checked to see if they had left on good terms or not. It goes without saying that most would have left despondent and with a grudge, potentially leading to severe grievances.

A further problem they had was that they were not familiar with the names, due to the wide range of nationalities. Some may have gone back to their homeland. So, tracking them down would be a challenge. Also, they needed to see whether there were any links to terrorist organisations. The special investigations squad would be able to help them with this.

The problem they had was they had limited time. If everything was going according to plan for the hacker, the next building was just about to go up in smoke.

Chapter 51

The original contractors who had designed and installed the BMS software system were called. However, as the maintenance contract had long been terminated, they had no interest in helping the cause. There was no love lost when it came to doing business in Dubai.

They then managed to get hold of the present contractor, Westminster Controls, who maintained the BMS software. They spoke good English, which was a relief to them, as getting Ausaf to translate anything technically related would have been a problem.

Alan Jones, the senior manager, dialled into the telephone conference call. Dan briefly explained the sequence of events, and the resulting fire. All Alan could say was, "oh my god."

Dan then said, "Alan, we have a serious issue here. We have a building that is on fire and it appears to be something to do with the BMS software, possibly a cyber-attack of sorts. Can you please give us some idea what's going on, and, more importantly, can you tell us how to fix it?"

"Dan, we were informed about the problem around an hour ago now, and our best

BMS engineer is trying to gain access to the building software. However, we are experiencing the same issue as the security manager had. We can't manually make any changes. It appears that the password and usernames have been changed or overridden."

Alan informed them, "The only people who had the master access to the software, who could override what the hacker is doing, are the manufacturers who are based in America."

He added, "The main issue we have is that the Americans, due to their time difference, are still asleep and it's going to be a few hours before we can contact them."

This information did not help their cause.

"Can you give us an idea what may be happening then?" asked David.

"Well, as we have no access to the software, we can't tell you exactly what's happening. However, anyone will tell you that if you switch off the A/C to the building, it will get hotter by the minute. Then possibly cause a fire when it got too hot."

"Who would have access to these passwords and usernames?" asked David.

"Well, most of our engineers, your local staff would also have these as well."

Dan then asked the question, "Your Company presently has the maintenance contract for these buildings. How do we know this wasn't caused by one of your staff?"

David added, "You see Alan, our engineers may have the passwords and usernames, however they don't have the knowhow to alter the underlying software programs. They have not been trained to do anything like this."

There was an immediate silence from the other side of the telephone. It was obvious that Alan had not considered this and was struggling to come up with an answer.

Alan tried to reassure them, "All our engineers are security checked, most had been working for us for years and they are all loyal employees. I would be surprised if any of our engineers did this."

This last fact was not entirely true, as most working in the BMS industry would tell you that there was a high turn-over of staff compared to other sectors. They worked long hours, and any employee loyalty was influenced by how much the next company was offering them. If they got a better offer elsewhere, they would leave swiftly.

David asked, "Give us an idea, say, over the past three years, how many software engineers would you have employed?"

Alan replied, "Phew, at a guess, I would say around fifty."

David looked at Dan and raised their eyebrows as they realised that this background check would take days, not hours. This wasn't what they had wanted to hear from Alan.

Dan enquired, "How many of our buildings do you presently maintain?"

Alan replied, "The numbers change all the time, as contracts are being constantly won and lost. I believe that we are looking after twenty of your buildings at the moment."

"Is each building looked after by only one of your engineers? Do we know who looks after the Arabian Gulf Plaza building?" asked Dan.

There was a moment of silence on the phone as they were trying to source this information. Alan then answered, "Only a few buildings have dedicated engineers. Most buildings, like the Plaza, would have mobile engineers, and whoever visits the building each day is randomly selected."

"How many times a month would they visit the building?" asked David, who clearly had no idea about the planned maintenance procedures of the building.

"The planned maintenance is carried out once or twice a year. However, if there is an issue, we would come out and carry out a reactive visit," replied Alan

"So," said David, growing frustrated, "how many different engineers would have visited the Plaza in the past three years?"

He replied, "Possibly eight or ten different engineers. Of which, some may have moved on to other employment."

"Can you please provide a list of engineers, past and present, who have visited the Plaza building in the past three years? Can we have this done a.s.a.p.?" he said in a firm voice.

Alan confirmed that he would do this for them. He then pointed out another potential issue. "Each of your buildings had different software systems, each maintained by different companies. To correct this third-party intervention, every software control manufacturer would have to be contacted."

Dan looked at David, and both raised their eyebrows, as this was not good news. Dan thanked Alan for his time and ended the call.

Dan turned to Ausaf, "Do we know which software systems are in all the different buildings?"

He replied, "No, we don't have a central database with these details."

Knowing that this was not the answer that Dan was after, Ausaf added, "We have over 50 buildings which most have these software systems. Also, when they are installed, it does not necessarily mean that they are with the building for life. They may be changed or upgraded along the way. It is impossible to know which systems are installed in each building."

Dan turned to David and said, "I don't believe this, these buildings are worth over $500 million each, yet we have no idea what software systems we have in place in each building. We have no strategy to prevent a cyber-attack from a malicious hacker. Anyone could hack these buildings and control them."

David added, "We could have, say two or three, cyber-attacks taking place at any one time, as we don't know when and where these are going to take place. Because there are different software systems in each building, each manufacturer would have to be contacted, so that the issue could be corrected."

Ausaf added, "A number of these manufacturers may have gone out of business as well." This was not what Dan wanted to hear. If there ever was a worst-case scenario, he had just heard it.

Dan looked at David and said, "Most of our buildings have security guards and a receptionist at the entrance. Most have metal detection equipment at the front door to prevent someone from coming through the door with a gun, or a small bomb. However, the possible business risk, the financial cost, associated with this intrusion at the front door, was nothing compared to a 'hack' into the central operating software system."

David said nothing but nodded to confirm this fact.

Dan added, "All the facts suggest that we can't stop this destruction of these buildings. The owners are going to have to pay this ransom, whether they like it or not."

Chapter 52

At 15.00, there was a sudden flurry of activity in the office as the special investigation squad had arrived. There were five of them, most had moustaches, and all wore sharp suits and the latest designer sun-glasses. It appeared that if you were in a position of importance, and you had an inflated ego, you needed to dress like a fictional character from the latest Hollywood movie.

David smiled, looked at Dan and said, "The men from the Matrix have just arrived." Dan smiled back.

As to be expected, it was customary for those in responsibility to not smile, and that the usual pleasantries, such as a greeting, were by-passed and all instructions were 'barked' at you. The words 'please', and 'thank-you', had been excluded from their range of vocabulary.

The head of special investigations was Lead Detective Rashid Amari. He looked younger than Dan had expected. It was obvious that whatever he lacked in experience was overcome by a desire to enhance his reputation. Dan spent the next fifteen minutes going through all the facts, and the entire sequence of events.

He tried to highlight the possible consequences if the owners did not pay the ransom, but he knew that the sophistication of the crime was lost on them. Rashid's immediate response was to send out instructions to man all front doors with extra security staff. It was pointed out to them that security was already on all the sites, and that all buildings were in 'lock-down' mode. Having extra security at the door would do nothing to prevent further fires. Dan added that all security staff have reported back and that everything was fine, that they had not seen someone walk in with a can of petrol and a box of matches.

When Rashid asked who could have done this, Dan replied, "It could be an external terrorist organisation or, either a present, or ex-employee, or an outside contractor." He then passed on the ACE Company's employee list to Rashid and said, "Here is the list of potential engineers who may have carried out the deed. Please can you run security checks through your database?"

Rashid looked at the list and then looked up saying, "This is not possible. This will take days to do a background check."

He added, "It would be easier to give you a list of possible potential terrorists who could have done this."

Dan replied, "Well, it's a start." Knowing that the whole exercise would be a futile waste of time and effort, but at least they would be seen to be doing something about it.

Chapter 53

The building engineer designated for the Arabian Gulf Plaza, was Fareed Khan, who was from Punjab in Pakistan. When one of Rashid's men knocked at his front door, they were lucky to find him home as he was just on his way out with an overnight bag. Whatever plans he had for the day were about to change for the worst for him.

He was loaded into the police car and transported over to the ACE offices. An empty room, alongside the emergency response room, was selected as a suitable venue to interrogate him and Fareed was directed to sit down.

He had a slim build, and was dark with a good crop of hair, parted to one side. He looked like someone who ate sparingly, not tempted by the excessive culinary indulgences of the western world. He would never have a weight problem and only needed fresh air and water to live on.

Fareed appeared nervous and agitated. He only kept eye contact for an instant before looking for some distraction so he could look elsewhere.

Rashid started the line of enquiry, "Fareed, are you the engineer at the Arabian Gulf?"

"Yes," he replied, looking at Rashid fleetingly and in a condescending manner.

"How long have you been working at the Gulf?"

"Eight months," he replied, looking away.

"Do you know how your building caught fire?"

He shrugged his shoulders, "I cannot tell you. It is my day off. I am not on duty." Once again avoiding eye contact.

"Are you concerned that your building has caught fire?"

He replied, "I was not on duty."

"Have you any idea how the fire started?"

His answer was short, "No."

"Do you have the passwords and usernames for the software controls?" Asked Rashid.

He replied, "Yes, all the engineers have those."

"Did you give your password and username to anyone else?"

"No," he replied.

"Fareed, my colleague tells me that when he came to pick you up, you were on the way out. Is this correct?"

"So?" he replied.

"Where were you off to?"

He took a moment to think about his response and said, "I was visiting friends."

"You had an overnight bag containing at least two changes of clothes and your passport. You also had two mobile telephones without SIM cards. Can you tell me what your plans were?"

He repeated, "To visit friends."

Rashid responded, "Most people don't walk around with two mobile telephones with no SIM cards in them. Can you tell me why?"

Fareed did not answer the question, nor did he bother to change his line of sight, as if he were thinking about something more important and had no need to respond.

His answers were short, loose, and vague. They lacked empathy, nor a desire to take responsibility. He appeared to have a 'don't care, so what' attitude, like a bored kid at school who isn't interested in some seemingly unimportant schoolwork. For most policemen, or customs officials, this 'not interested' attitude when interrogating an individual was infuriating and suggested that they had something to hide.

It appeared that the 'softly' line of questioning was not working, and that a different approach was needed. Dan looked at David, they both smiled as they knew what was coming next.

Rashid, in an instant, stood up, towering over Fareed, slammed the table with his fist and shouted. "Did you start the fire? Who are you working for?"

Fareed was caught off guard, he looked back at Rashid, and then Dan, in shock before composing himself. Gazing down toward the floor, he delayed his answer, "No."

Rashid, still towering over him, raised his voice again and said, "Did you give the access user password to anyone?"

Once again, Fareed, did not meet his stare and said nothing.

Dan was wondering what was coming next. Was he about to witness Rashid give Fareed a beating, something he'd remember for the rest of his life? Dan was not sure that he wanted to be in the room when that happened.

Dan was not sure whether Fareed was hiding something or just had a resentment of all authority, or perhaps the evils of western society that were not in-line with his religious beliefs.

Having worked at the Arabian Gulf for a period meant that Fareed had a good understanding of the comings and goings of the building, and knowledge of the mechanical systems. However, his overnight bag did not contain a laptop which would have provided access to the building software.

If he had started the fires via a laptop, it meant that whilst he was in custody, there should not be any further fires, which would be a relief for the owners.

He did have the building software access passwords. Could he have passed them over to others either for financial gain or for more sinister reasons? Perhaps he had passed them to a terrorist group to cause the destruction? His lack of detailed answers meant that they were forced to speculate. But Fareed was the only suspect that they had for now.

There was a knock on the door, and the help-desk coordinator beckoned Dan outside for a message.

Chapter 54

At 16.00, another text message came through to the ACE help-desk, and it was from the local security manager at the Marina Towers building. Dan looked at the message and it read:

'The Marina is getting hotter by the minute. I have had to evacuate the building. The controls are not working. Please advise.' signed Abdullah, the Security manager.

The Marina Towers Buildings was the second site to be targeted by the hacker. It was another high-rise commercial building, located about five miles from the Arabian Gulf Plaza and situated on the bay, overlooking the gulf. It had thirty floors of luxury offices and had a multi-tenant occupancy. Where the Plaza was over thirty years old, the Marina had only been open for five years. It was one the owner's recent possessions, one of the most prestigious buildings ever built by the Emirates group. It had cost an estimated $700 million and if anything was going to get their attention, it was the destruction of one of their latest properties.

The text caused an immediate outbreak of shouted instructions from Rashid to the special investigation team.

Dan noted that there was this local perception that the louder the instruction, the quicker the orders would be followed. Or, out of fear of reprisal, the action would be definitely carried out. What the locals couldn't understand was that it did not matter how loudly they shouted, there was nothing they could do.

Rashid instructed two members of staff to head immediately towards the building to investigate. Or possibly, to put out the fire themselves, all on their own. Rashid then contacted the city fire department, and another shouting match took place. A senior director of the fire department was finally brought to the phone, and he made it clear that most of their fire fighters were already at the Plaza. It was then pointed out to Rashid that they only deal with building already ablaze, as they couldn't extinguish a fire that hadn't even been lit yet.

This fact had bypassed Rashid. All it had done was wound his pride and made him even more aggressive towards his junior members of staff.

For the next thirty minutes, Dan and David went through the facts with Rashid again, highlighting to him that there was nothing that they could do. They had to convince Rashid, and the owners, that the only solution was to pay the ransom. They pointed out that $100 million was a bargain compared to $1.2 billion that was about to go up in smoke. Yet, it did not matter what they said, Rashid remained stubbornly blind to the facts.

All he could say was, shaking his head, "You pay the ransoms in America. In Dubai, we don't pay terrorist groups." Rashid was convinced that it was a terrorist group carrying out the destruction of the buildings. Even though it was pointed out to him that this may be too sophisticated an operation for a terrorist group. And that, typically, terrorist groups didn't demand a ransom. These facts did nothing to deter his line of thinking.

Rashid then instructed a member of staff, one with good knowledge of computers, to track down the location and user of the phone that had sent the original warning text. Hopefully, they would then be able to find the contact details linked to the registration of this mobile.

A short period later, it was confirmed that the text could not be traced. It had been sent from a pay-as-you-go SIM card and was not registered to anyone. The phone was switched off after each message was sent out. So, tracking or tracing where the message had been sent from would be impossible. Whoever was sending the messages could simply send a message, then drive to the other side of the city, then send another.

Rashid said thoughtfully, "Fareed must be that person. He had two mobiles that had no SIM cards in." He added, "Did he dispose of the SIM after the last telephone exchange?"

A number of telephone calls took place between the owners and Rashid, once again in a language that Dan couldn't understand. After each call, Rashid would not tell them what had transpired. He was obviously keen to tell the owners of the latest development, hoping that he would get the credit for a positive outcome. He was deliberately keeping them in the dark, refusing to pass on valuable information.

Dan turned to David and said, "In the land of the blind, the one-eyed monster is king." David smiled back at him in agreement.

Dan was trying to work out what had influenced his decision to not inform them what the latest was. Was it his ego, his stubbiness, his potential loss of reputation or just his lack of intelligence? Either way, it was not helping the investigation.

Whilst all the above was taking place, Dan had asked the ACE HR department to check if Fareed had worked at the Marina before. A short time later, it was confirmed.

Prior to working at the Arabian Gulf Plaza, Fareed had worked at the Marina for a year.

Dan turned to Rashid and David and relayed the information, "Gents, it has been confirmed that Fareed has worked at the Marina. It is time to speak to Mr Fareed again."

This latest news to Rashid was good to hear, and a large smile broke out on his face. "It must be Fareed. We have our man," He said, looking around the room and waiting for confirmation from the others.

Chapter 55

Dan and David re-entered the interrogation room and sat down opposite Fareed, who had not bothered to look up at them.

Rashid came through the door next, with an attitude like John Wayne entering a saloon and making as much commotion as possible, hoping to ensure that everyone knew that he had arrived.

He got straight to the point.

"You worked at the Marina before. Yes?" answering his own question before Fareed could answer. Dan was sure he saw Fareed smirk, when he heard the name, as if to acknowledge some kind of achievement.

"The Marina is now on fire. Do you know anything about this?"

Fareed said nothing and continued his attempt to look disinterested.

"So, you don't want to talk?" Once again, Rashid gave Fareed no time to answer, if he had even intended to.

Fareed never answered back.

Rashid decided that he was going to get no information this way, and that he was wasting his time. He then half-turned to his assistant and nodded.

The assistant, who was a giant of a man, an ex-bodybuilder, produced a pair of handcuffs, then attached them to Fareed's hands. He grabbed Fareed's shirt above his shoulders and semi-pulled him off his chair. Fareed had no option but to follow him out of the door. Fareed was to be delivered to a local police station where the interrogation would continue.

At the station, the interrogation would be less talk, more physical persuasion.

Chapter 56

Around 16.30, Westminster Controls supplied Dan with a list of ten engineers who had visited both the Arabian Gulf Plaza and the Marina Towers in the past three years. Their CVs indicated that two came from Dubai, three from India, two from Pakistan, two from England, and one from the USA.

Dan figured that, as this attack could well be motivated by terrorism, he should focus on the engineers from Dubai, Pakistan, and India. His gut feeling was that the English and American engineers had no access to the local terrorist groups, so were unlikely to be involved.

From the list of engineers, seven were still employed with the local companies and living in Dubai. There were three on the list that appeared to have either moved onto other employment, or returned to their country of origin. The missing people consisted of two Indians and an American.

The list was passed onto Rashid for his department to investigate the names on their databases to determine if there were any links to terrorist organisations.

Rashid, seeing the list, turned to Dan and asked, "Why are you interested in this list. We have our suspect?"

Dan replied, "Do we really have our suspect? He has not confessed to anything. We have no evidence to confirm he was responsible."

David supported his colleague, "If he were the suspect, he would need a computer to start the fires. Where's his computer?"

This fact appeared to have slipped Rashid's mind.

Within the hour, local detectives had visited these ex-employees and they were each on the way to the police station for interrogation.

Chapter 57

At 18.00, another message was passed onto Dan. It read:

"The Marina Towers building is now on fire. There is nothing you can do. Please pay the ransom if you want to prevent further fires."

Dan stood up, picked up the binoculars, swung around and pointed them into the distance. As there were so many high rise commercial offices in Dubai, finding the Marina was not easy. But once Dan had located the smoke, billowing out of the side of the buildings, he knew which one it was. His immediate thought was, "There goes another half a billion up in smoke."

He turned to the rest of the occupants in the room, the blood draining from his face, and said, "The Marina is now on fire." He passed on the binoculars to whoever was keen to observe the impending destruction.

Abdullah, the Marina security manager, was called and he confirmed that the sequence of events was identical to before. The second building catching fire was no coincidence, and whoever was hacking into these buildings was serious.

With each message that they received, they now knew that if it were reported that a building was getting hot inside, within a few hours the building would be ablaze. As each message was read out, it felt like a train crash taking place in slow motion. They knew that it was going to happen, they could see the outcome, but they couldn't do anything to stop it.

The confirmation of the second fire was a sense of relief to most in the room. Up until this point, their plans were based on speculation, on 'what-if' scenarios. With no evidence, they realised that with each passing hour, there was nothing they could do to change the course. They were stuck in this helpless situation, hoping that it was a sick joke. Even after the first building had caught fire, they still did not believe that the second building would burn. Now that it had taken place, they knew that the original warning text had been real.

The starting of the second fire took place around five hours after the first one, and now two very expensive buildings in the Emirates Real Estate portfolio were ablaze. With an estimated financial loss of collectively $1.2 billion in assets, it was obvious that the owners had no other option but to consider paying the ransom.

The main issue obstructing the investigation was that this was not a working day, so any essential information that could have potentially helped them was unavailable. Also, the fires were set so quickly that they had no time to investigate potential suspects. Furthermore, having Rashid in the room only made things more difficult.

Dan turned to Rashid, and once again, highlighted that $100 million was insignificant when compared to the $1.2 billion going up in smoke. If the ransom didn't get paid, this damage could get worse. Still, Rashid refused to accept the facts.

He spent his time pacing the office, back and forth. The routine was an attempt to portray that he was formulating some master plan, something to solve the problem and boost his reputation with the owners.

David's patience was at a boiling point, likely due to his Yorkshire upbringing, where fools weren't entertained. He looked at Rashid and raised his voice, "Do you really think you can solve this without paying the ransom? This problem is not solvable, you can't fucking fix it."

He added, "Tell the owners to pay the ransom now, before more buildings go up in smoke."

The room went deathly silent. David had crossed the line. Nobody challenged Rashid's orders. However, it needed to be said. The charade that Rashid had been playing had progressed to a point of no return. Unfortunately for Rashid, David had a temper that was equal to his. David was also considerably larger than Rashid. Furthermore, David did not care if he lost his job. He was not one of the locals who were willing to do anything out of fear of losing their jobs.

Rashid gave David a very intense stare that would have scared most grown men. The confrontation was just about to escalate, when Dan stepped in, hinting to David that it was time for a cigarette break, managing to somewhat diffuse the situation.

Chapter 58

They entered the lift, descended down to the ground floor, and were soon outside, facing the harsh heat. Dan had given up smoking years before, but when his stress levels were off the scales, he resorted to some nasty, man-made chemicals for some relief.

Whilst outside, Dan turned to David and asked, "Have you ever experienced anything like this?"

David replied, "I would rather be chasing some psychopathic serial killer in Halifax than this."

Dan, having never been to Yorkshire, did not fully appreciate David's point. Still, if what he was described was worse than this, then it must be a pretty bad place.

David added, "What makes it worse is that we have to deal with Rashid, who has the emotional intelligence of a ten-year-old."

Dan smiled and nodded his head, "Yes, that doesn't help."

When they got back to the emergency response room, they were joined by the owners, who had just arrived.

The owners, who Dan had never met before, were dressed in traditional dress with the customary robe and headgear. The intensity of the conversation increased and Dan and David, along with any other English speaking employee were left behind while the discussion was conducted in the local language.

To impress the owners, Rashid had now taken over the management and direction of the investigation, constantly pointing to the incident board and going through the sequence of events. This was his time in the spotlight, presenting to the owners what he had done and what the strategy was.

The owners, turned to Dan, and in broken English, asked him to give them his opinion. Dan spent some time going through potential outcomes and pointed out that there was very little they could do.

He pointed out to the owners, "We know how the fires are starting, and we have a potential suspect, but we still don't know what their motive is."

"If no more fires take place, then we know that we've stopped the threat, and that Fareed is linked somehow."

He added, "But we still do not know where the money is going. Once we know where the ransom is being sent, then we can trace it and track down who is doing this."

All they could do was wait for the next instruction.

The main question on everyone's lips was whether there would be more burnt out buildings before they were told where to pay the ransom. Also, having paid the ransom, would they stop causing more fires to the other buildings? All they could hope for was that Fareed was responsible for this mayhem.

The owners still showed no signs whether they intended to pay the ransom or not.

Chapter 59

Around 20.00, Jim McAvennue, the General Manager at the Dubai Sheraton, received a text message on his phone. As Jim saw the text, his heart almost stopped, it read:

'Your hotel is now under our control. It will catch fire in one hour.'

"Holy Jesus," he said out loud in his Irish accent, "those bastards have decided to take over my hotel."

A few minutes before, he had noticed that his office was getting warm, and he just about to look into it. He immediately looked at the building management screen on his PC. The temperature in his room read 25°C, and it was increasing. He tried to adjust the setting, but to no avail.

He immediately phoned the ACE emergency response room, and Dan took the call.

Jim, sounding distressed, said, "Dan. We have just received a text message informing us that the hotel has been taken over."

This news came as a shock to all occupants in the emergency response room at the time. The Sheraton was the next building targeted by the hacker. The hotel, another building in the Emirates Real Estate portfolio, had 500 rooms with numerous conference rooms, swimming pools, and other facilities that you would find in any luxury hotel. The building was over 20 years old but was still regarded as one of the most prestigious hotels in Dubai.

The fact that the hacker was now targeting buildings that had occupants meant that he was turning up the heat, taking the threat up another notch. The lives of the general public were now under threat and they, as a company, would have to be seen responding to the situation. Any deaths resulting from their inaction would not help their reputation.

Dan's immediate reply was, "Jim, is the building temperature increasing?"

Jim responded, "Yes, it has definitely risen and it's starting to feel hot. I have tried to turn it down, but nothing is happening."

The owners intervened, "Jim, get everyone out of the hotel now."

Jim replied, "I am instructing my staff now to that now."

Jim headed straight for the reception area where he instructed the senior management staff to evacuate all guests and visitors. He then headed towards the conference room area where a very important event was taking place, the annual diamond auction, a highly prestigious event on the social calendar for the Dubai elite.

Chapter 60

Unbeknownst to most in the ACE emergency response room, the annual congregation of local billionaires, as well as a few poor millionaires, was taking place at the Dubai Sheraton on that night. They were there with their wives, partners, and some with their Russian supermodel brides-to-be.

The annual event was a small, private affair for the select few, by invitation only. There were much larger diamond auctions that took place in Dubai that attracted the rich and famous from all over the world. However, this event was a more exclusive affair for those who wanted to be discrete about their purchases and who didn't want their privacy broadcasted to the masses. Much like a secret poker school, it had started small and then grew over the years, and the event was only known by this secret group, who wanted to keep it that way.

Diamond traders and only the top designers from all over the world were invited to the auction. For them, it was an opportunity to make some real money. The show-stopper designer piece was estimated to sell at $1 million, which was the starting price. The auction was unique as it was the only time that this group of billionaires would congregate in one place. It was an opportunity to see who had the biggest ego, and who could out-bid the other.

Around 18.00, a small buffet with drinks was held outside the conference hall so that some socialising could go on before the serious event took place. All the talk at the time was about the two fires that had happened over the afternoon. Some at the auction had significant investments in the Emirate Real Estate group and were understandably concerned.

As the Sheraton hotel was part of the Emirates Real Estate group, there was good reason to be concerned that it could be the next target. However, the thought of missing the annual auction would be too much to bear, especially for their partners. The senior management had assured them that all security precautions had been considered and that evacuation plans were in place if needed.

Around 19.00 they all proceeded towards the auction area, and once padded down by security, they were shown through the metal detectors, which allowed them into the confines of the area. Along the perimeter of the conference hall was a row of tables, where the exhibitors had their diamonds on display. They were allowed to approach the eager dealers and designers, to peruse the collections of cut and uncut diamonds before the auction was due to begin.

Many potential factors determined the value of cut and uncut diamonds, such as clarity, colour, shape, and size. However, in most cases, the wives and partners of these wealthy people were the ones who determined the value, typically inflating the costs. The dealers, working in cahoots with the auctioneer, knew this and were keen to make sure the value of their diamonds was far greater that it would be anywhere else.

At 20.00, the auctioneer for the night beckoned everyone to take their seats as the auction was about to take place.

It was around this time that the temperature in the room started rising, rapidly approaching 25°C. Most of the occupants at the auction started to feel restless and hot.

Jim suddenly appeared at the entrance to the auction, before proceeding to the stage. He took over the microphone that the auctioneer had been using.

"Many apologies for interrupting the auction. I need to inform you that we have just received a threat informing us that the hotel has been taken over."

He added, "it appears to be the same threat that was directed to the Plaza and Marina Towers buildings this afternoon. We need to take this seriously as the hotel may catch fire. Can you please head for the exit and congregate in the hotel car park."

Most people experience a range of emotions in their life, including shame, guilt, greed, and fear. The fear of fire is one of the worst and most common fears out there, as burns can result in extreme pain, disfigurement, and an excruciating death. Everyone had seen the images on TV that afternoon, and had felt the increase in temperature in the room. So, thinking that their lives were in danger, they immediately panicked and stampeded towards the door. Their self-preservation was their only priority at the time.

The dealers and designers, who were well aware that they were being asked to leave their diamonds worth millions behind, turned to Jim and explained their predicament. Jim reassured them that the area would be locked after the last person left, which he would personally do, and that the hotel would be responsible for any financial losses. He explained that the conference area was separate to the main hotel, so should not be affected by the fire.

Within a few minutes, all the guests and visitors had left the area. Jim had a final look around the auction area, and seeing that no one remained, locked the door and proceeded towards the car park.

All the hotel guests and visitors for that night were soon congregating in the car park, waiting for the fire to take place.

Chapter 61

Back at the ACE Emergency Response room, Dan called the HR department again and asked if Fareed had worked at the Sheraton before. Everyone in the room sat in eager anticipation, staring at the telephone, waiting for it to ring and confirm that Fareed had worked indeed at the Sheraton.

HR came back in ten minutes. Dan picked up the phone and spoke with the caller. The call was short and brief.

Dan put down the phone, turned to the others and said, "Fareed has never worked at the Sheraton."

They all looked back at Dan, expressionless, their balloon well and truly deflated. Their recently obtained lead in the investigation, their one and only, was suddenly heading in the wrong direction.

David added, "If Fareed hasn't worked at the Sheraton before, then who has taken over the hotel?"

Dan replied, "Well, obviously not Fareed as he is in custody and he has no computer to start the fire."

For Rashid, this was not the news that he wanted to hear. He banged the table, standing up, and shouted out some obscenity in the local language likely, an offensive word used to express displeasure.

His immediate reaction was to make another call to the police station where Fareed had been taken. He gave further instruction, still using the local language. Dan had no idea what was said but could assume that it would result in a further beating for Fareed, whether he deserved it or not.

"Could there be more than one person? Is this a group who've obtained the software passwords from a number of ACE building engineers?" asked David.

Everyone in the room heard the question but did not bother to answer him. They did not want to think about the consequences of such a theory being true.

Chapter 62

At 21.00, another text message came through to the ACE help-desk and passed on to Dan. Dan read out the message:

'Please pay the ransom of $100million to The Green Climate Fund (GCF). This demand is unconditional and any attempt to renege the financial transaction will result in further destruction of your buildings. If this ransom is not paid by 22.00, we will destroy your other buildings. Do not inform the media or the general public of this payment.'

The Green Climate Fund, set up by the United Nations, was the world's largest fund dedicated to helping developing countries to reduce their greenhouse gas emissions and to enhance their ability to respond to climate change. Where local governments needed financial support to tackle the devastation of climate change, such as extensive flooding, the GCF would step in and help-out. For poor countries, whose citizens would be affected the most, this aid was a life-line.

For any commercial property developer in Dubai, discussing the subject of Climate change is the worst thing you could mention in a conversation. It was like throwing a pork sausage in a synagogue, the ultimate sin. It meant that they had to comply with additional regulations and follow building construction compliance. It caused the construction costs to increase. It also prevented them from showing off their importance, their self-indulgence, which meant that their dreams, their master plan of creating the spectacular, were held back. It was like taking a favourite toy away from a child.

Paying the ransom to the GCF was the last thing they would dream of doing. For the locals, who had no sense of humour, it was like an awful joke. They would rather have paid the money to the Emirates retired hooker's pension fund, rather than the GCF. The part of the agreement banning them from broadcasting their generosity was also an issue. If they had to do it, they wanted to make sure that they got the maximum amount of exposure, so they could show off their perceived green credentials.

At 22.00, back in the emergency response room, the Emirates group owners finally relented, and the ransom was paid. The GCF, who were not in any way aware of what had happened, were more than happy with the $100 million injection of cash into their coffers.

For the members in the emergency response room, the news was a relief, and a weight of expectation had been lifted from their shoulders. For Dan, it felt as if someone had simply switched off his stress button. All the anxiety that he had been experiencing had disappeared in an instant. He looked at David, and they both knew what it meant, another cigarette break was needed. The cigarette was a celebratory one, not a stress relieving one.

Chapter 63

Once back in the room, Dan looked at the investigation board. Under the 'Who is doing it' section, they now knew where the money was going. But they still did not know who had carried the attack out.

Would the GCF, or someone representing them, have actually hijacked these buildings and set them on fire?

The GCF were a highly respected organisation whose intentions were to help humanity, and to prevent future poverty for those who needed it most. Most would confirm that they would not be associated with these crimes. If exposed, or linked, their reputation would be forever tarnished. The climate change non-believers around the world would have had a welcome boost to their beliefs that the theory, and supporting studies, must be false and the threat didn't exist.

Could someone have carried out the threats, then donated the ransom? A good Samaritan who miraculously gives away $100 million? Was this revenge, a form of retribution, from a group of anti-capitalists? Could they expect further attacks of a similar nature, robbing the rich to help the poor?

The thought was hard to accept, but there was so much resentment against the greed of the rich, that it could easily be true. The size and sophistication of these events suggested that it must have been a group who had a strategy in place, their practices carried out by a group of well-educated individuals.

For all in the room, they just hoped that paying the ransom would mean that all further fires would not take place.

Chapter 64

At 22.00, whilst everyone waited in the Sheraton car park, waiting for their next instruction, Jim received another text message. It read:

"The ransom has now been paid. Your hotel has been saved. It will not catch fire. Your guests may now go back inside."

Jim, upon receiving this instruction, experienced a sudden relief that his hotel was not about to go up in smoke. He turned to his key members of staff and instructed them to re-enter the hotel with him to confirm that the temperature had indeed dropped, and to check if any fires had taken place. Inside the hotel reception, it was apparent that the temperature was back to normal, and a quick scout around, revealed nothing out of the ordinary.

He returned to the car park and, with the help of a loud-speaker, informed all guests and visitors that the threat had passed, and they could go back into the building.

Jim followed everyone back inside, reassuring everyone who still had reservations about re-entering the area that it was okay. He then proceeded to the conference room area, where there was a congregation of restless people wanting to get on with the auction, and some who were keen to check that their goods were still in place.

Jim took out the key and opened the door, and stood back, to allow everyone to re-enter the area. In an instant, there was a loud cry from within the area.

"Where are my diamonds?" shouted one of the dealers, soon to be followed by numerous others.

By the time Jim had re-entered the conference area, there was a chorus of disenchanted dealers and designers demanding that Jim tell them what had happened to their diamonds.

Jim looked at the tables of empty displays. It was obvious that the diamonds that were previously there were long gone.

This was soon followed by others in the room complaining that their credit cards were missing from their wallets and handbags.

The blood drained from his face. "Sweet holy Jesus," he thought, "we have been raided by a group of robbers who must have stolen the contents of the auction."

He looked around the room, trying to look for an obvious reason why the diamonds could have mysteriously vanished. He looked at the stage door, but that was still firmly shut. There were no obvious signs of forced entry. They had just, disappeared, into thin air.

His stress levels were increasing by the minute, due to the number of very irate people all pointing fingers at him and threatening him with various accusations. It was pointed out that the last thing that he had said was that the hotel would take full responsibility for any loss. He suddenly regretted his reassurance at the time, knowing that it was going to prove to be something he would regret for the rest of his career.

The mayhem extended for some time, before Jim could remove himself from the area and get free of the abuse directed towards him. He headed back to the inner sanctum of his office. He closed the door, and thought, "could anything in my life get any worse than this?"

Jim headed towards the drinks cabinet and poured himself a large whiskey, slugged it down in one, and then poured another. This provided instant relief but was no real help as he knew that his next action was not going to go down well.

He phoned the ACE emergency response room for the second time that night, and he was put through to Dan.

He informed him, "Hi Dan. A diamond heist has just taken place in one of the conference rooms. It appears that whilst we were all out in the car park, someone stole all the diamonds and some people's belongings."

"Holy cow," was all that Dan could say. He turned to the occupants in the room and relayed what had just taken place at the Sheraton. They all looked at each other in disbelief.

For the past ten hours, they had experienced a rollercoaster of bad news, and now they have just been informed of a diamond heist that had taken place on one of their properties. They had hoped that once the ransom had been paid, their nightmare would have gone away. How much more bad news could they expect?

Dan regained his composure and came to the quick conclusion that he had to prioritise his efforts. He said, "Jim, as you may expect, we have enough on our plate to deal with. We don't have the resources to help you at the moment. As this incident involves the public, can you and your security team sort this out? I will come around in the morning first thing."

Jim hoped that he could have expected some support from his head of group security. However, he realised that Dan had too much to cope with already. The thief of a few million dollars worth of diamonds was not in the same league of the billions that had just gone up in smoke. At least his hotel never went up in smoke, he thought.

For those in the room, the news of the diamond heist on one of their properties was the last straw. You could feel the tension in the room. Everyone was shell-shocked, with nothing further to offer to the conversation. Some had heard enough and decided to retire for the night.

Chapter 65

Dan worked long into the early hours of Saturday morning. He managed to finally escape from his office, and he found a local hotel to catch some sleep, knowing that he was expected back at work at 07.00 again. He knew that the day would be a long one, full of meetings and shouting matches. Everyone trying to apportion the blame onto others, desperate to absolve themselves of responsibility, regardless of the facts.

He woke up and had a quick shower, then put on his sweaty clothes that he had been wearing the previous day. Dan had yet another stressful day ahead so he skipped breakfast, he had other important things to deal with.

He was not headed straight to the ACE office. He instead had to visit the Sheraton hotel, as he had promised Jim the previous night.

Investigating a diamond heist would give him some relief from the relentless events of the previous day. It also meant that he had an excuse to not see Rashid and his team for a few hours. He could imagine them scheming and plotting how they could apportion the blame onto him, asking why he never reacted sooner, and finding whatever other perceived incompetence that could be pinned on him.

Whilst driving his car across town, Dan was surprised that even during all the drama and action that the two fires had caused, they had still been notified that a diamond heist had taken place. Could it be possible that the two were linked, or was it just a coincidence?

On his way, he drove past the Marina Towers. The top half of the building was completely destroyed and now only a shell of mangled steel and brick. The fire fighters were still there, trying to douse what embers remained. The legal ramifications and the long-term financial loss of the fire would go on for years and amount to billions of dollars.

He reflected on how easy it had been to take over the building, cause the fire, and then switch it off when the owners had paid the ransom. All this damage was done from someone's laptop, perpetrated by an invisible person, and nobody had any idea who was responsible, or from where.

When Dan arrived at the Sheraton, he parked his car and then proceeded through the main reception and onto the GM's office, where he found Jim. After some brief introductions, Jim told him about all that had happened during the previous evening.

They then both walked towards the conference centre, which had been taped off by the local police to restrict access to the crime scene. There were a number of policemen there, some taking fingerprints, others, interrogating the hotel staff. There were also several angry diamond dealers who demanded explanations for the loss of their diamonds, explanations, and reprisals that had been guaranteed by the hotel management. Most had already instructed their lawyers to proceed with seeking compensation for their loss, which would cost the Sheraton corporation millions, if the insurance company refused to pay out the amount.

Dan asked Jim to confirm his movements before locking the door.

Jim replied, "I was standing at the door, and I saw all the occupants leave the area. I then re-entered the space to make sure that everyone had left. When I saw no one was in the area, I closed the door and locked it."

He added, "I am 100% sure that there was no one left behind in the area."

Dan asked, "Any CCTV in the area?"

Jim replied, "We have CCTV located outside in the corridor. I have had a look at the recordings, and they confirm that no one entered the area whilst we were outside in the car park."

He added, "We have no CCTV in the conference area."

Dan smiled back at Jim, "It would have been a big help if we had," stating the obvious.

Both Jim and the local head of police, agreed that they had no idea how the theft could have happened. Dan walked around the conference room and surveyed the surroundings. He looked up at the ventilation systems and saw that a person couldn't have fit through the ducting grille. He noted that there were only two doors, the main entrance, and the back-of-stage-door. Could the thief, or thieves, had entered through this back-of-stage door?

He walked up to the back-of-stage door and tried to open it. Dan turned to Jim, "Where does this door go, and why is it fastened closed?"

Jim responded, "The door is the entrance to the back-of-house area. It has been fastened closed for the past five years now. The area is used for storage and I don't believe anyone has been in there for ages. "

Jim added, "The only entrance to the area would have been through the front door."

Dan needed to investigate this further and see where this door went, and what existed on the other side. Dan asked Jim if he could check the back-of-the house area. Jim instructed his head of hotel security to show Dan the area.

They walked out of the main entrance, then around the side of the hotel until they reached the conference area and the emergency exit door for the back-of-house area. The head of security sourced the master key and opened the door. With a push of the door, they entered the space.

It was dark, and once the light switch had been located and switched on, they could see what the area contained. Dan made his way through the narrow space to the interconnecting door, which would have led them into the conference area. He tried opening the door, but it was securely fastened. He surveyed the area around the door and found the four screws that held the door firmly to the frame.

His first thought was that this looked similar to a case he had worked in the past, the Rivonia Casino heist. He remembered that the thief had screwed the access hatch closed, which had prevented him from discovering important evidence that could have helped him solve the crime.

Could it be possible that it's the same person? He smiled, and wondered at the chances of two people from Harrisburg, living and working in Dubai at the same time It would have been impossible, too much of a coincidence.

He looked at the screws and thought, "If the person had a key to the exit door, and a portable screwdriver, these screws could have been removed in minutes. This would have given them access to the auction area, and to the diamonds that were on display."

As he could not think of any other way the robbers could have entered the space, he was sure that this was the only entrance into the crime scene last night. The only people who had the key to the external door would be senior members of the hotel staff. This looked like an inside job to him.

He left the area and soon re-joined Jim in his office. Dan explained what he saw and his theory of how a thief could have entered the area.

Dan said to Jim, "The CCTV shows that no one entered the main door. So, the heist could have been only carried out using the back door."

He added, "If this is this case, then they would have needed the exit door key, or the hotel's master door key. One of your staff members would have access to these keys. They would have known that a diamond auction was taking place, as well as the layout and where the internal door led to."

He surmised, "Jim, this looks like an inside job to me, possibly with some help from an outsider, or group."

Jim looked at Dan in shock, but he had to accept that there was merit to Dan's theory.

He said, "Yes, this is Dubai," he smiled, "I'm sure that a member of my staff could have done this." Dan smiled at the comment, agreeing with the sad indictment of the locals, knowing that it could be true.

"However," said Jim, "we got a text saying that the hotel was just about to go up in flames. Are you saying the group that burnt down the Plaza and Marina Tower were also responsible for the diamond heist?"

Dan responded, "To tell you the truth, I am struggling to link the two. It may just be a coincidence, or that with the drama unfolding in the afternoon, the thieves used it all as an excuse to execute the heist." Dan recognised that he was speculating, and the potential link all sounded strange to him.

He did not believe that the average diamond thief knew anything about building software controls or ventilation systems. The fact that they both took place at the same time further suggested that they couldn't be linked. How could they be in two places at the same time, he thought?

Dan asked Jim, "Can we have a list of all members of staff, past and present, who had access to these keys."

Jim responded, "Yes, that's not a problem. Give me an hour or two."

Dan, knowing that he had more important issues to address, turned to Jim, and said, "Jim, as I am sure you can appreciate, I am presently trying to investigate the Plaza and Marina Towers fires. This robbery involves private citizens and would have to be investigated by the local police." Jim nodded, feeling some sympathy for Dan's present workload.

Dan added, "Can we please pass this onto the person heading up the investigation. But keep me in the loop, just in case there is a link between the two."

With that, they both got up and headed towards the hotel reception doors. Dan finally shook Jim's hand and promised to keep in contact.

Dan had barely moved a few meters, when a thought crossed his mind, curiosity getting the better of him. He turned towards Jim, and called out, "Jim, sorry, one more question," sounding like a scene from a Columbo TV series.

Jim responded, "of course."

"How many engineers do you employ and where do they come from?"

Jim mentioned that he employed around five engineers, all coming from various nationalities.

Dan asked, "Do any of the engineers have an understanding of BMS software controls?"

Jim looked at him amazement, and said, "Yes, our head of engineering has a BMS background."

Dan smiled and replied, "What's his name, and do you have any background on him?"

Jim responded, "His name is Nigel Hunt, he's from the USA, and he used to work at Westminster Controls. He joined us around three months ago now. He is a nice, genuine guy and I find it hard to believe that he'd have done this."

"Where is he now?" said Dan, thinking that this may be the first sign of evidence that they may have.

"Well, he took his annual leave last week. So, he might not have been around last night." Replied Jim.

Dan asked, "Do you know where he lives?"

"Yes, he lives in the staff apartments that the hotel provides."

Dan said, "Can we go there straight away?"

"Of course." Said Jim.

Jim called over the head of security and asked him to take Dan to the staff apartments. Dan said goodbye to Jim for the second time.

Dan and the head of security both walked to the hotel car park and climbed into their cars. Dan followed the head of security to the staff apartments.

The supervisor, who looked after the daily operations and cleaning of the apartments, met them when they arrived. They parked the cars and climbed the stairwell to the third floor, to the apartment where Nigel Hunt lived. They knocked on the door a few times, and when they realised that no one was coming to the door, the supervisor used the spare key to open the door for them.

They entered the room to find no one at home. A quick look at the wardrobe suggested that Nigel Hunt had moved on from the apartment. Neither the supervisor, nor the members of the hotel staff, including Jim, had been told about Nigel's sudden departure.

Dan looked around the apartment to find it was bare. It appeared that Nigel Hunt had given it a good clean before leaving, and he left no potential evidence that could have been used in the investigation, should he be the potential suspect.

Heading back to the car, Dan gave Jim a call, and informed him of his findings. Dan then asked, "Have you got any photo identification of Nigel Hunt?"

Jim, replied, "I'll get hold of HR and see if we can get you a photo. However, it may be tomorrow as they have Saturday off."

Back in the car, Dan started thinking. Nigel Hunt knew about the auction, had experience in BMS software controls, and had previously worked at Westminster Controls. All of this suggested that he was their main suspect. He had also disappeared into thin air, further hinting that he could have committed the diamond heist. But what about the building fires? Could Nigel Hunt have been responsible for both crimes?

He was sure that the documentation that Westminster had sent over, had described an engineer who was an American citizen, however, at the time, Dan had never bothered to register his name.

He had a positive lead, and they had a name, Nigel Hunt.

PART 3

Chapter 66

After the Ravonia casino heist that he had successfully pulled off in Harrisburg five years ago, Greg Johnson had spent the two years living on Anna Maria Island, a small island located near the city of Tampa, on the west coast of the USA.

The island had an 'old-world' charm as no major retail corporations had invaded the area yet. The locals were fiercely proud of their independence, providing an enclave from corporate obsesses that the USA had to offer. As he knew that the FBI still had him on their radar, it was a convenient place for Greg to hide out for a year or two. He blended in with the locals, while making sure that he never befriended anyone. He kept his own company which was what he preferred.

Greg had rented a small apartment, owned by an old lady, to whom he paid his monthly rental bill in cash. This one-off amount covered all his electrical costs, along with any other associated rates. As he didn't have to register his rental to the local Utility service providers, Greg had no traceable payment records.

He also decided not to purchase a car, or register for any taxes, as Greg knew that this was a sure way to attract the attention of the FBI, or any other police force potentially after him. If you had a car, it meant that most databases would have your name. Every driving offence that you had gave you a record for life, and they always knew where you lived. His main objective was to avoid possible detection from the authorities, and he knew that he had to side-step all contact databases.

Using the 'dark' web, Greg managed to find someone who could give him a false identification. This involved money, but soon Greg had a new ID and a passport under a new name. One that was not traceable by any government authorities.

He spent most of his days swimming, keeping fit and visiting a local sports bar to watch whatever sports event on at the time. With time, Greg realised that he was procrastinating his life away, and he needed to change his newly adopted lifestyle.

Greg decided to enrol with a local College course in Tampa, which he attended a few days per week. The course was engineering related, which was what he enjoyed doing, and it was a Building Management System software course. BMS, as it was commonly abbreviated, was the software that controlled the heating, ventilation, and air-conditioning in the building. It made sure that the heating system did not operate during the summer, nor the air-conditioning in the winter. Most large commercial buildings have a BMS in place to control many day-to-day operations, such as the tenant comfort levels within the building. It was a popular qualification for anyone who wanted to progress from being an electrician or plumber, to a position that was more intellectually challenging.

The college were well aware of his dyslexia and they provided the facilities to ensure he completed the course. Having completed the course, and with his recently acquired qualification, Greg joined a local company called Westminster Controls, which had an office in the Tampa area and specialised in the design and maintenance of these BMS systems. The company was a global company and had offices in most major cities in the world.

After two years working for the company, he proved to be a very competent BMS engineer, helping to design and maintain these systems.

One day his boss called him in and asked if he would be interested in a new position that was on offer. As he was still single, with no apparent family commitments, they figured that he would be interested in the position. It was for a BMS position located in

Dubai. The position was well remunerated and came with a number of perks. Greg, with over half a million dollars to his name, thanks to his earlier successful casino heist, was not that interested in the money that was on offer.

His immediate thought was that it was a good way of getting out of the country for a few years, that is, if the FBI were still investigating him. Furthermore, as he had never done any international travel, it was an opportunity to broaden his horizons. A simple search on the internet showed that Dubai was a glamorous place, with good weather and a high-standard of living.

As much as he enjoyed life on Anna Maria Island, Greg decided that it was time to move on. He accepted the job, and was soon on his way to Dubai. Upon arriving in Dubai, Greg felt, for the first time in the past few years, as though he wasn't being watched or that he had to look over his shoulder. He enjoyed the freedom that was on offer and it meant he could be a free man again.

Chapter 67

Westminster Controls in Dubai had a number of high-profile clients and they looked after over two hundred commercial buildings. Greg's job was to look after the BMS control systems of several large-scale commercial buildings owned by the Emirates Real Estate group.

With time, Greg built up a reputation and was highly sought after. Although he enjoyed the work, the lifestyle in Dubai was fast and furious with a demanding working environment. He, and many others who worked there, soon came to resent the local way of life and the heavy hand of the law enforcement aimed at any foreigner. It appeared to be one rule for them, one for the foreigners, and the locals seemed arrogant, thinking themselves better than anyone else.

He noticed that Dubai was one of the worst countries in the world for inequality and the whole system was built on inflated egos and men with the emotional intelligence of children. Everything had to be bigger, better, and glitzier. People acted like teenagers in the showers showing their more impressive penis off to everyone else. The whole charade was built on borrowed or stolen money.

Retribution Man

He could never understand the logic why anyone wanted to constantly make more, and more, money. Making a million was never enough, it had to be a billion. He couldn't see the point. When one died, money meant nothing. When you arrived at the cemetery gates, being the richest person meant zilch and you had definitely proved that you weren't the wisest. Passing on all this money to the family simply meant that their children would grow up completely divorced from reality, never having to work and living in this cocoon of the super-rich, only obsessed with their security and their self-importance.

Greg was an American, so he knew all about financial greed and the obscene obsession of chasing after the 'American dream'. He had been brought up in a society where 'more was good', that 'greed was good', that there was only 'one winner' and screw all others. This all created immense inequality, where the average citizen couldn't even afford the basics such as health care or decent education for your children. If you couldn't afford basic health care, there was always the threat that you were going to die to something entirely preventable, earlier than someone who was better off.

Those, like his mother, desperately tried to make ends meet, and to provide a decent education for their children. As a child, Greg could never remember if they ever went on holiday. His mother had worked her whole life doing two jobs, and had never experienced a holiday. If you couldn't experience the nice things in life, like a holiday, or you couldn't treat yourself to a spa treatment, then your whole life must be crap, he always thought.

The local Emirates elevated this obscene greed culture to another level. Their whole existence was based on greed, and it did not matter how you achieved it. There was no such thing as a moral compass and showing any form of empathy was a sign of weakness. The winner takes all, everything was all about massaging their over-inflated egos. They made the American elite look like amateurs.

The commercial buildings in Dubai had to be bigger and better than any other major city. These temples, a status symbol to those who owned them, stood high and proud, a perfect way to show off how amazing they were and to prove that their egos were bigger and better than everyone else's. The only way to get respect was by being wealthier than the next person. For those at the bottom of the food chain, life consisted of working excessively long hours, with an hourly rate which was barely enough to live on.

The migrants were all treated like modern day slaves on a massive scale. They were all slaves to these assholes, and they all needed to be grateful for them as they were giving their lowly slaves a job, an opportunity to serve these masters of the universe.

One of the frustrations that Greg experienced was that there was no loyalty shown by senior management, or the building owners. It did not matter how hard you worked; at any one time you could lose your job. Everyone in Dubai lived with the fear that they were next, and that they would not have a job to go to in the morning. That was how the owners of these buildings wanted you to feel, as it meant that they could manipulate you to do whatever they wanted. This included working long hours, six days a week.

Every morning. Greg woke up thinking about it and it made him sick. Over time, this anti–establishment, anti-capitalism, attitude built up within him, along with his resentment at the inequality of the system. He wanted to take revenge in his own way, the only way that he knew how. It was time for retribution.

Chapter 68

Previously, most commercial buildings had a resident engineer responsible for the daily operations, making sure that the ventilation systems and the lights worked. The majority of the work, and adjustments that were carried out onsite were the responsibility of the local engineer. However, when Smart Building Technology came along, it revolutionised the type of services that the sector could offer.

Smart Building Technology was all about computers and IT software system controls. These systems were now the chosen technology to be installed in the latest buildings. All the mechanical and electrical systems onsite, which controlled the ventilation, cooling and heating, and the lighting and fire extinguisher systems were now all controlled remotely. There was a marked movement away from a manual labour type service towards an outsourced one, driven by technology. The overall objectives of these systems were to save maintenance costs, energy costs and most importantly, on labour costs.

One of the issues with Smart Build Technology, however, was that the technology was way too advanced for the average building engineer. You now needed to have an understanding of computer programming, as well as building services engineering. As most of the engineers were from the Philippines, India, or wherever they could get cheap labour, the introduction of this technology was going to leave these people behind.

What this really meant was that the buildings were now completely managed and operated by third-parties. Where previously, the owner might have had some control of the building by employing their own staff, everything was now completely outsourced, as yet another cost-cutting exercise. This also exposed these buildings to outside influences and possible cyber-attacks if in the wrong hands.

When this technology came along, Greg found himself in the right place and time. He was soon part of the new revolution and he embraced all the latest technologies, making sure that he was familiar with the software and how to reprogram these systems if needed. As he had helped to install these systems into ten buildings in the Emirates Real Estate portfolio, he had valuable background understanding of the buildings and how they operated. This knowledge would prove invaluable in the plan that he had in mind.

Chapter 69

Whilst Greg was driving to work one morning, he thought about how easy it could be to take over one of these buildings and hold the owners to ransom. He had the tools and the knowhow to make it happen. The more he thought about the very simple plan, the more he liked it. It was like the Rivonia casino job he did five years earlier, a perfect opportunity to seek revenge on the elite, those rich bastards who made people's lives an unpleasable, meaningless experience.

The plan was simple. Most of the external walls of these commercial buildings were made of glass. By midday, with outside temperatures reaching over 50°C, these buildings had the potential to turn into infernos, at least, if they had no air-conditioning to cool them down. The solar gain into the building was immense and all the energy that needed to operate the air-conditioning had little to do with tenant comfort levels but was primarily to control the solar gain and prevent the building from overheating.

He couldn't understand why anyone would design and build a building made of glass. These buildings were like massive greenhouses, generating excessive heat during the day. It was all for the vanity of the owners as glass buildings looked more appealing than boring brick-built ones, so screw the environment and the amount of energy that it took to keep them cool.

The incoming fresh air to the building, which could be as high as 50°C, was treated with air-conditioning to maintain 20°C in the office space for the tenants to work in. If a building didn't have these large energy consuming air-conditioning systems in place, the tenants would fry, so to speak.

As Greg had the master usernames and passwords to access these buildings, his plan was to log into these buildings, remotely, via his laptop, and then change all the access codes for the software. He would then switch off the air-conditioning systems. He would still operate the ventilation systems however, as the incoming air hadn't been cooled down, the internal temperature would soon match that of the outside.

The planned sequence of events would have to be done on a Friday, a non-working day in Dubai. His main concern was that, on an ordinary working day, there was a risk that some of the tenants could die from heat exposure. Furthermore, Greg knew that if no specialist contractors were working, it would be almost impossible to contact anyone who could solve the problem. Even if they managed to source the original manufacturer of these systems to correct the issue, the time zones would make it much more difficult to sort the systems out.

Having switched off these systems, he would then monitor the increase in internal temperatures. He knew that within thirty minutes, the internal temperature would be the same as the outside, 50.C. With the help of the midday solar gain, and with limited air in the building being extracted, this would result in the internal temperature rising further still.

In a few hours, he would expect the internal temperatures to approach 80 to 100°C. The electrical wiring had an upper limit of 70°C before it started melting. So, when the internal temperature reached this point, the plastic covering on the electrical wiring would start to melt and the exposed wiring would come into contact with other wiring, making it arc and causing an electrical fire in one of the areas in the building.

Greg was not entirely confident that a fire would actually light in the building, but the excessive heat would prevent anyone entering the building, so he still had control of his plan. The plan being getting the owners to pay the ransom, before he cooled down the building again.

Furthermore, Greg also had control of the fire detection and extinguishing systems for the building on his laptop, so he would just switch those off. This meant that if there was a fire, it would not be detected or extinguished, as most systems are designed to do.

This could all be done by giving his laptop a simple instruction and then pushing the 'enter' button on his keyboard. As he had changed all the usernames and password access protocols, there was nothing that the local building management staff on site at the time could do to correct the issue. Even if they could, the high temperatures in the building would drive them outside.

Even when the local fire department arrived, there was not much they could do. Trying to extinguish a fire on the 15th floor would be impossible. Also, entry into the building would be unbearable for a human, at potentially 100°C.

To control the whole process, Greg could switch back on the air extraction and air-conditioning systems, and this would soon bring the building core temperature down to a lower level. To stop the fire, he could also switch the fire extinguishing systems back on, soon extinguishing the fire.

As he had the BMS access software codes for at least twenty buildings within the Emirates group, Greg could decide which building he wanted to ignite at any one time. From his laptop, he had access to all of these building systems software. Potentially, he knew that over $5 billion in assets that could be destroyed in hours.

In his mind, Greg constantly challenged his motive for carrying out this plan, this destruction. He did not consider himself anti-capitalism, or anti-establishment. It had more to do with inequality, the treatment of fellow human beings by these rich bastards who thought they were better than the next person. It was against those who showed no empathy for others who happened to be less fortunate. It was for all the hard-working slaves, like his mother, who had to pamper to these assholes. Retribution would be sweet.

For the owners, it wasn't about the money. Greg knew that he was stoking the fire of something much bigger, their ego, their self-importance, and their vanity. Seeing their buildings going up in smoke meant that their empire was crumbling down in front of them. Their perceived status in the community, and their business reputation was at stake, all of which was more important than money to them.

The owners would have no option but to pay the ransom. What he liked about the plan was that he did not need anyone else's help. Not like the Rivonia job, where he had to hire and then kill the two thugs who he had needed to help him carry out the heist.

Chapter 70

Six months before the Friday of the building fires, Greg had been instructed to carry out a modification at the local Sheraton hotel, owned by the Emirates Real Estate Group.

He had been told to install the latest SMART building software that was needed to upgrade the BMS system at the hotel. Greg spent a week at the hotel, taking full advantage of the generous hospitality on offer and greatly enjoyed his time there. When he had first come to Dubai, he had been told that if a job at one of the luxury hotels came available, it was well worth considering for the many perks that came with the position.

Besides the free food, the large hotels in Dubai provided accommodation for their workers and free travel to and from the hotel. The free accommodation was located only five miles from the hotel. In Dubai, the only cheap accommodation was found in the distant suburbs, which meant commuting three hours every day, which Greg resented. For him, this was the main attraction of working for one of these hotels.

Whilst he was working there, he saw a position advertised for a Head of Engineering. He got on well with the general manager, Jim

McAvennie. When he had a chance, he asked Jim what the job entailed. He was informed that they needed an experienced engineer with air-conditioning and ventilation background. As Greg had experience with this type of work previously, he asked if he could apply for the job. He added that the hotel would get a free BMS man thrown in as well. Jim, knowing that he was getting a good all-round engineer, gave him the job straight away.

Greg was tired of working for Westminster Controls. Although the work was interesting, his workload on an average day was hectic and he was constantly asked to do more than possible. Besides more money, taking up the offer meant that Greg could progress his career into an engineering management position.

Upon taking the job, he soon settled in. The job was more laidback and there was a relaxed working environment. He soon met a Filipino lady, and his evenings became filled with passion and lust.

Three weeks before that eventful Friday, Greg was called into the General Manager's office for the usual morning briefing. He was told about an important function that was due to take place, it would be a diamond auction held in one of the smaller conference halls. This was an annual event, for a small group of billionaires of Dubai, and not to be missed by the selected few.

The security on the night was critical, and the last thing that the hotel wanted was for a heist to take place while the auction was taking place. As head of engineering, Greg was to meet with the main organisers of the event and go through the final security checks.

A few hours later, Greg met with the head of security, Ahmad Omar, a local coming from a military background. As the event was now in its twentieth year, Ahmad had a good idea of what preparation was required for the event. Ahmad explained the procedure on the day, the extra requirements that would be needed from the hotel staff.

The entrance to the conference room was to be protected by heavily armed security guards, all highly trained ex-military men. Besides the bag checks, to be carried out by Ahmad's men, a metal detection machine was to be installed at the entrance to ensure that no guns would be allowed into the area.

Whilst walking around the conference room, Greg noticed that Ahmad was fairly relaxed about the event, which suggested that the previous events had taken place without any major incidents. To Greg, it appeared that once the security arrangements were in place, there was little else for the hotel engineering staff to do.

The conference room, smaller than the rest, was typically used for corporate functions and it held around fifty people. On one side was a small, elevated stage where the main presentation, the auction, would take place. The construction of the stage had been an afterthought, and behind the stage was a narrow back-of-house area where the electricity control boxes for the sound and lighting systems were located. Many years previously, this interconnecting door had been fastened securely, so that no one was allowed in or out of the area. Due to how it was designed, the door was secured from the back-of-house area.

When alone, Greg, who had never seen the back-of-house area, decided to explore the area so he walked around to the outside of the conference area and found the exit door to the area. Seeing that it was secured by a lock, he removed the master key from his pocket, inserted the key, twisted it, and the door opened.

He entered the space, sourced the internal light switch, and switched it on. At the far end, Greg could see the interconnecting door which would take him through to the conference area, and he made his way through the narrow passage. He noticed that there were some spider webs, and that everything was coated with dust, suggesting that the area had not been entered for many years.

Upon arriving at the interconnecting door, he noticed that the door had been fastened together to the frame with four screws, located at each corner. Greg was not sure what he had expected, but he was sure that the door would have been more securely fastened. It would have been near impossible for somebody to open the door from the inner room. However, from Greg's side of the door, a common screwdriver made accessing the door a simple procedure.

Greg smiled, finding the mentality of the local Emirates hard to believe. A diamond auction was about to take place, and if anyone had wanted to carry out a heist, all they needed was the key for the external door and a screwdriver to open the internal back door. The front door to the conference would be so heavily guarded that not even an elite army battalion could infiltrate the area. However, the most obvious risk, the entrance through the back door, was inexplicably overlooked, seen as unimportant.

It had not been considered as a potential issue as, from the inside, the door was secure, unable to be opened. But nobody had bothered to walk around the building and open the door to explore what was in the area.

A smile suddenly broke on Greg's face, as he had just come up with a plan to carry out a diamond heist.

Chapter 71

With some planning, Greg decided that Friday the 17th of August, was the day to execute his plan. A simple search on the internet gave him the ACE FM out of hour's help-line desk.

On the day, at around 12.00 am, Greg opened up his portable computer, entered his username and password into the Emirates Real Estate company portal, and then selected the Arabian Gulf Plaza building. As each building had its own unique password that was common for all to use, he proceeded to change the master password. He was now the only person who had access to the building software.

He switched off the air-conditioning systems that provided the cooling for the inner office space. He also disabled the fire detection and extinguishing systems for the building.

Having previously helped to convert the Plaza building to Smart Building Technology, he knew that it was one of the older buildings in the portfolio. As his plan had never been carried out anywhere in the world to date, Greg had to prove for himself that it was possible. By starting off with the older building, if his plan did not work, he could simply walk away. However, there was no logical reason why his plan should not work.

He also switched on his non-traceable, pay-as-you-go mobile, and sent his first message to the ACE Facilities management help-desk. It contained the warning and the ransom demand. Once sent, he switched off the mobile, so nobody could track his location.

Using his laptop, Greg then monitored the building's internal core temperature for each floor. As expected, the floors at the top of the building rose almost instantaneously. Within thirty minutes, the internal temperature was now up to 50°C, the same as the outside temperature. He could imagine the local building security manager trying everything to bring down the temperature. As he had no access to the software controls, he would eventually be forced to leave the building, as there was no way to correct the situation.

The entire time while this was taking place, Greg was sitting in Paddy's Irish Bar, his favourite sports bar, having a beer and a bite to eat. He logged onto the internet and located the YouTube app, where he then sourced the live web stream for the downtown area for Dubai. The Plaza building was in the line of vision of the cameras. He was waiting for signs of the first fire taking place.

Around 13.00, he noted that the inner core temperatures had increased to 70°C. An hour later, the first fire appeared on the 15th floor. He picked up his mobile, switched it on, and then sent off the second text message, notifying ACE that they had a fire at one of their buildings.

Having seen the consequences of his actions, Greg was spurred on to see his overall plan through. It was frightening to notice that he had all this power to determine if a building was destroyed or not. Greg was going to make the owners pay for every man-hour it took to build these preposterous temples.

Chapter 72

Around 14.15, Greg decided to implement the second stage of his plan.

The Marina Tower building was the next building on his list. He knew that if the owners hadn't taken him seriously the first time around, they would now know that his threats were real. He also knew that the Marina was one of the newer buildings and they would be outraged at any destruction.

It was like playing a psychological game with the owners. He first decided to set ablaze one of their oldest buildings, the Plaza, knowing that the building was already near the end of its shelf life. The owners may have chosen to take the insurance money and look at it as an opportunity to rebuild another monstrosity in its place. However, the Marina Towers fire was a more recent building, and this would have significantly hurt their ego.

Greg knew that the latest building would always be their favourite, the shining beacon in the portfolio, the chosen one. Then, as soon as the next project was finalised and ready to build, this new building became the favourite. It was like a child having a favourite toy, until the next one comes along.

The destruction of the Marina Towers Building would go straight to the heart of their vanity, their self-importance. If the Marina building went up in smoke, it would be a serious injury to their pride, like a dentist hitting an exposed nerve. As their reputation in the Dubai commercial real estate world was diminishing by the hour, the owners would have a serious decision to make.

Once again, Greg went onto his laptop, logged onto the Marina Towers portal, and carried out the same procedure as he had before. Within minutes, he noticed the increase in inner space temperatures. On each occasion, the building took around two to three hours, from start to finish, to be set alight.

At 17.00, when the Marina finally caught fire, Greg switched on his mobile and sent another text message to the ACE facilities help-line, informing them that they had another fire to deal with.

By the time the Marina had finally caught fire, the local fire department had not one, but two buildings that they needed to extinguish, that is, if they could even get anywhere near the buildings.

The second building had more of a media impact than the first with the general public. The TV cameras were already broadcasting live at the Plaza, when the second building caught. They soon sent another team across to the Marina Towers. The local and foreign, press corps were aware of the fires and, when the Marina went up in smoke, rumours were starting to spread that it could be a terrorist attack. It was like seeing 9-11 taking place again, the demolition of the Empire State Centre buildings in New York. The owners, having seen the constant repeat of news, were now going completely berserk as their egos had been well and truly deflated.

Around 19.00, Greg left Paddy's Irish bar and set off for the Sheraton hotel. He arrived at the hotel car park around 19.30. Sitting in his car, he decided it was time to implement stage three of his plan. He opened up his laptop, selected the Sheraton hotel, and increased the local temperatures in the hotel areas to 30°C.

Unlike before, he had no intentions of causing a fire at the hotel. There were too many guests in the hotel at the time, and the last thing he wanted was to be responsible for causing a guest's death. Besides, he had enjoyed his time working at the hotel, and had made some friends. He did not want his actions to result in them losing their jobs, as the consequences of the fire.

Soon after, Greg noticed that the internal temperature in the various areas increased immediately. He then picked up his mobile and sent his first text to Jim

.

Chapter 73

Greg had a clear view of the entrance to the hotel, and he saw all the comings and goings taking place. He soon saw the car park filling up with the hotel evacuees. He smiled as he watched the outcome of his actions, witnessing the mayhem that was taking place. His master plan, which had only taken a few days to put together, was soon to become real. He casually climbed out of the car and proceeded towards the hotel.

To avoid any detection, he was dressed in his working uniform with a cap, and he carried a small over-the-shoulder bag. He walked down the side of the hotel that took him to the side entrance of the conference room, where the auction had been taking place. Within a few minutes he was alongside the emergency exit door. He quickly looked around to see if anyone was about, and then opened the door with his master key. Once inside, Greg found the light switch and then closed the external door. He approached the connecting inner door to the auction area. He took out his portable screwdriver and unscrewed the four screws that held the door securely to the frame.

He cautiously entered the space to find it empty, as he expected. The heat inside the area was around 30.C and was just bearable. He knew that the longer he stayed in the area, the more unbearable it would get. The displays, which showed off the diamond collections, were still lying in their place. Greg went over to each one and scoped up the contents with his hand, before placing it into his bag. He did not remove all the diamonds, and he left some of the designer 'show-stoppers' behind. They may have been traceable when it came to selling the items on.

Within five minutes, most of the diamonds had been relocated into his bag. Greg then looked around and noticed that a number of handbags and jackets had been left behind, still hanging over the previously occupied chairs. He quickly went through each bag and jacket, looking for any wallets. He removed only the credit cards. He hadn't expected to find these credit cards, but he had a good idea of what he was going to do with them.

The heat in the room was starting to get unbearable and he was soon drenched in sweat, it was time to leave.

He exited the conference room, the same way he had entered. He stopped to replace the screws in the door to how he had found them before. He switched off the internal light, then opened the emergency exit door to find that no one was around. He closed and locked the door. Then, with his bag over his shoulder, Greg casually walked to the front of the hotel and back to his car in the car park.

He walked past the hotel guests, billionaires, and dealers, who were all waiting for the fire to start. Some were desperate to get back into the auction area to retrieve their belongings. They were venting their frustrations to anyone prepared to listen to their plight. He got into his car and drove off back to his apartment.

The whole heist had taken place over just 20 minutes. There had been no guns, no evidence left behind, and he did not believe that he had been seen. So far, so good he thought.

Chapter 74

The trip back to his apartment took around thirty minutes. Looking around the Dubai skyline, he could see two buildings on fire in the distance. Once safely back in his apartment, Greg opened his laptop and logged-on to the Emirates group portal. He first switched on the fire detection and extinguishing systems at the Plaza and the Marina Towers. He also switched on the air-conditioning systems, just in case they weren't too damaged to work.

He then opened the Sheraton Hotel portal and lowered the space temperature back to 20°C so that it was bearable for guests to go back inside. He sent his last text message to Jim informing him that the ransom had been paid and it was okay for them to go back into the hotel.

He proceeded to retrieve the contents of his bag, the diamonds. He had previously purchased four hard-covered Bibles. He had cut out a rectangular hole within the Bible pages, removing the internal section. This left him with a secret compartment, around the size of a small lunchbox. He placed the diamonds into the compartments and closed them. To ensure that the Bible could not open, releasing the contents, he then shrink-wrapped the Bibles with plastic.

He placed the Bibles into four prepaid, air-post envelopes addressed to a hotel in Barbados, where he was intending to spend tomorrow night as a guest. In the declaration section, the contents of the envelope, he wrote Bibles. Under the recipient section, he wrote down the Church of Apostles, Bridgetown. Hoping that this would fool any immigration officer that may be more than curious about the parcel. Greg didn't know that there was close to $5 million worth of diamonds in those envelopes.

He then removed all the credit cards from his bag and proceeded to photograph both the front and back of each. When complete, he then transferred the images from his phone, via Bluetooth, onto his laptop and then into a folder he had created.

He signed himself onto the 'dark-web', which he joined as a member a few years ago, when he had purchased his passport. He prepared a simple email message. It said:

'Gents, please find attached the credit card details of some well-known billionaires in Dubai. Enjoy".

He then compressed the folder containing the credit card information and attached the folder to the email message. He then pressed the send button and in an instant, the credit cards were now in the hands of the twisted morons of the dark-web.

Unbeknownst to him, within a few minutes of sending the message, there was a frenzy of activity, like sharks gorging on the bloody carcasses of a few billionaires thrown into a pool. Before he had left his apartment, hundreds of thousands were being siphoned off their accounts, never to be seen again.

Sending this email was a deliberate ploy of his as when the crime investigations started, there would be a link to these people, so the investigation would focus on them.

Greg removed the SIM card from his mobile phone. The SIM card that had given him the tools to cause all the mayhem and destruction of the past twelve hours. He took out a box of matches, lit a match and placed it under the card, which caught fire instantly. The ashes fell onto the kitchen sink, then were washed away. In an instant, any evidence that could have linked him to the scene of the crime was now gone for good.

He had a final look around the apartment, making sure that there was no evidence left behind. He then set off for Dubai airport, stopping along the way to post his four envelopes in a local post box. He also dumped his mobile into a nearby bin.

Chapter 75

An hour later, Greg was passing through the Dubai airport immigration section. He was soon sitting in an executive bar having a well-earned beer. He was watching the local television news stations which were covering the scenes of destruction. Dubai had never seen or experienced anything like this.

As there was still no mention of a ransom demand, the various TV pundits were still speculating which terrorist group could have carried out the fires. The local journalists were in overdrive, with a non-stop input of ideas and possible scenarios, all provided by 'so-called' experts on the subject. It was their turn in the spotlight and with every new suggestion of the possible cause, there was another opportunity to expand and explore the story even further.

There was no mention of the hotel diamond heist yet.

At 01.00, he boarded the international flight to the Bahamas. Sitting in first class, with a glass of Champagne in his hand, he reflected on the day that he'd just had.

Within twelve hours, Greg had caused a loss in assets for the Emirates group of close to $1.2 billion and stolen around $5 million worth in diamonds. He had also, indirectly, robbed a number of billionaires of a large amount of money on their credit cards. The total amount would never be determined.

He hoped that he had managed to boost the GCF bank account by $100 million. However, as all communication between ACE and him were all one-way, he had no idea whether the ransom had been paid, or not. As his final message had insisted that they could not broadcast their payment to the GCF, he would never know. Yet, Greg was more than confident that it had been paid. The possible threat of the destruction of further buildings would have influenced their decision to pay the ransom.

Once he had found someone to purchase his diamonds, his plan was to give most of his proceeds to the homeless, those less fortunate in communities around Harrisburg. Retribution had been his main motive, and this would give him the most satisfaction of all the destruction he had caused.

Greg looked forward to a good night's sleep on the aeroplane and, upon arriving at his destination, a long swim in the hotel pool.

Chapter 76

Dan, whilst driving back from the Sheraton to his office, realised that he hadn't eaten since lunch the previous day. As it was lunchtime, and he was desperate to have some time to collect his thoughts, he headed off to a local Bar & Grill that he frequented, Paddy's Irish Bar. He walked into the restaurant, found a seat, and ordered a burger and two beers.

He gave David a call and told him of the new evidence that he had just come across.

He asked him, "David, can you please open the document folder, the one that was given to us by Westminster Controls, containing the IDs of the BMS contractors?"

David carried out his instruction while on the phone, and when he came across the folder, asked Dan, "Which one are you looking for?"

"I want the ID of the American."

David confirmed, "The building engineer from American is called Nigel Hunt. "

"Bingo." Said Dan, "I think we may have our man. It appears that he may have carried out the fires and the diamond heist at the Sheraton last night."

David responded, "Well, he has been a busy boy then."

Dan asked him, "Can you take a photo of Nigel's ID picture and send it to me, via your smartphone."

"Yes, sure," replied David.

A few minutes later, he heard a 'bing', notifying him that a message had come through on his phone. It contained an attached image, which he then opened. The face that looked back at him was that of a slim, well-groomed man with black hair. He had a large smile on his face.

Dan had a close look at the picture, and in an instant, he recognised the person. His face had changed, as he looked slimmer than before and previously he'd had a beard. But the smile gave his identity away. Dan was convinced that this was the fire-starter of the buildings, and that he had carried out the diamond heist.

His name was Greg Johnson, the person who had carried out the Rivonia Casino heist five years ago. Dan knew what Greg was capable of, so figured that if anyone could have pulled off both the arson and the diamond heist, he could.

The two beers arrived, and he took a long mouthful. The contents tasted good and relaxed him in an instant. He took another look at the picture and smiled. Greg Johnson, alias Nigel Hunt, had been in town. He could not catch him the first time around, and he would be surprised if he could catch him this time.

Dan faced a dilemma, as a policeman he would have an obligation to investigate the crime. Should he declare to Rashid and his band of merry men that he knew who had started the fires and carried out the diamond heist? However, Dan was employed in the private sector now, for a company that was a contractor for the Emirates Real Estate group, so he had no obligation to divulge this information. The company that he worked with would not adversely be financially affected. In under a year, when the present FM contract ended and was up for renewal, they would be discarded, just like every other one they had entered.

He reflected on what had taken place and thought that what Greg had done was not really a crime where the general public would be affected. He chose to start the fires on a local holiday, when he knew that no one would be in the offices. The only people who were adversely affected were the billionaire owners of these buildings and a few diamond dealers. All he had done was bruise a few inflated egos. With all their money, and with the help of their insurance policies, they would soon repair their self-esteem, their business reputation, and move on and build something even more extravagant.

Furthermore, he had no sympathy for the locals, especially not the owners showing off their obscene wealth, making everyone work like a dog for minimal pay with poor working conditions. His time and experience in Dubai meant that he had as much resentment towards the locals as Greg. There would be no love lost on the day Dan left Dubai.

The fact that the ransom went to The Green Climate Fund, would suggest to most that Greg was a modern day Robin Hood, robbing the rich to give to the poor, or to causes that were more worthy than someone's self-importance.

In a strange way, Dan felt some sympathy towards him, they had a secret bond, and they were both local boys from Harrisburg. They were both from a city only famous for local government corruption and the extreme poverty experienced by the local citizens. A place where you were all doomed to live for the rest of your non-existent life. He knew of no one who had managed to escape, to seek new ventures, and go on to live a more fulfilling, meaningful life. Even if it included becoming a modern day Robin Hood stealing from the rich, making them payback for the misery that they inflicted on those less fortunate.

What Dan could not understand was why Greg did not claim the ransom himself. Then again, a ransom of this large amount was electronically traceable. Although he had carried out a sophisticated crime, there was a good chance that he did not have the knowhow to hide the money in an untraceable, off-shore bank. He was, after all, just a heating and A/C man, not a banking expert with a degree in accounting or IT, or whatever it took to make these arrangements happen.

Then it occurred to him, were the building fires just a distraction, a smoke screen for the real event? By the time the auction was due to take place, he knew that the fires that took place earlier would have been on the minds of most of the attendees. The images on TV were graphic, and fear of fire would have consumed their thoughts.

When the attendees had felt the temperature in the building increase, and then when the GM came in and told them to evacuate, their natural instinct would have been to rush to the door. Even the diamond dealers, having had the reassurance from the GM that their diamonds would be safe, would have headed for the exit door. No one wanted to be caught in the fire and burnt to death.

There was a good chance that the diamond heist could not have taken place without the building fires having taken place, he thought.

For most professional thieves, diamonds are the chosen prize due to their size versus financial value ratio. A small, pea sized diamond could be worth five to ten thousand dollars. The small item meant that you can simply slip it into your pocket, so they could be easily smuggled or transported, and there was always someone willing to purchase your illegal gains. Once in the hands of a professional diamond cutter, any traceable evidence disappears for good.

Similar to the Rivonia heist, Greg had created enough diversions so that when he carried out the ultimate prize, everyone was too busy fighting fires, or trying to work out what the hell was happening. Furthermore, there was no DNA left at the scene, no guns, no deaths, and limited evidence to work with. As the whole sequence of events all took place in a short period of time, it was impossible to link or catch anyone. In a typical crime case, it would take time and patience, usually extending into months, and they didn't have this luxury.

Rashid and his team may eventually manage to link the two crimes with a building engineer called Nigel Hunt. However, they would never know his real name, which was Greg Johnson. This meant that any in-depth investigation into his past would come up with nothing. Dan was the only person in the world who knew that Greg Johnson existed, and that he was linked to both crimes.

It was only the four screws, which he had been looking at on the back of the stage door that morning that had made his subconscious mind start working overtime, indicating that he had seen this pattern before. It was only his curiosity that made him ask Jim about the engineers that he employed at the hotel.

It was only Greg's smile on his ID that provided the evidence that linked the crimes, and that highlighted his identity.

It was not worth bothering to try and find him as Dan knew that Greg would be long gone from Dubai. Knowing him like he did, Dan was almost sure that Greg would have obtained a new name and identity by now. There was no limit to what that man was capable of.

"That boy from Harrisburg is a genius," he thought.

With a smile on his face, Dan decided not to report him.

He beckoned over the stewardess, who brought over another beer.

THE END

About the author:

Shaun's passion for writing started late in life and he is frantically trying to catch up for the lost time. He acknowledges that writing praises and accolades are limited at this time. However, going forward, he is hoping to change this.

Shaun's first book, 'The Rehab Weight Loss Plan' has won wide acclaim for its fresh and intuitive approach to the confusing quagmire of diet advice on our bookshelves.

His latest book, Retribution Man, is one man's revenge on all the inequality in the world. Delves into the underworld of the casino business, the excesses of Dubai real estate, and the shady characters it attracts. It is a fast paced page turner of a novel and likely to be the first in a series.

When he is not writing books, he is a mechanical engineer specialising in the field of energy conservation and sustainability, single-handily trying to save the world, one degree at a time.